IMMINENCE

IMMINENCE

◆ Nessumsar Family ◆

LEGEND OF THE CROW

DEBBIE IHLER RASMUSSEN

M.O.M.M.
PUBLISHING

Mysteries of My Mind

Published by:
M.O.M.M. Publishing
"Mysteries of My Mind"

Teenage Mutant Ninja Turtles
Created by Kevin Eastman and Peter Laird; Owners Mirage Studios and ViacomCBS

Beta Reader: Dottie Ihler
Cover Design: Dee Loupeti • www.deegraphics.net
Interior Design: Francine Platt • Eden Graphics, Inc. • edengraphics.net

979-8-9851721-2-6 Paperback
979-8-9851721-3-3 ePub
Library of Congress Number: 2023916096

Second Edition
Manufactured in the United States of America
10 9 8 7 6 5 4 3 2

DEDICATED WITH LOVE TO:

*My kids and grandkids —
you are ALL Superheroes to me!*

XOXOXO

OTHER BOOKS
BY DEBBIE IHLER RASMUSSEN

THE MYSTIC TRILOGY:
Mystic Angel
Mystic Lake
Mystic Mansion

MYSTIC TRILOGY BACK STORIES:
Best Friends Don't Leave
Sometimes Love Just Isn't
A Life of My Own (coming Oct 2023)

NESSUMSAR FAMILY—
LEGEND OF THE CROW:
Book I

CHILDREN'S BOOK
I Think My Grandma is a Witch!!

SPECIAL THANKS TO:

All my grandkids for being my characters in this series.
Special thanks to Axle for the gaming lesson ☺

NESSUMSAR FAMILY

PARENTS: Tiago and Brooke Yellek
Mack – *Shapeshifter; super strength*
Haydee – *Hear other's thoughts*
Harley – *Controls the element*

PARENTS: Emmett and Tatiana Yalc
Katie – *Invisible*
Kitana – *Invisible*

Janae Nietsnibur
Grant – *Hears thoughts, projects thoughts*
Ava – *Move objects/makes them appear*
Zion – *Runs at lightning speed*

PARENTS: Biorn and Antika Nessumsar
Spencer – *Invisible; super strength*
Brighton – *Fly; super strength*

PARENTS: Richard and Amanda Nessumsar
Nate – *Invisible; shapeshifter*
Samual – *Hears thoughts, projects thoughts*
Lock – *Shapeshifter*

James and Alice Nessumsar
Alex – *Runs at lightning speed*
Audrey – *Move objects with her mind*

Mayajaal – Training Island in Belize
Team Leader – Special Agent Mont Gunderson – aka Gunner

TEAM ASSIGNMENT
Operation Purloin

California
Handler – Char
Mack, Spencer, Ava, Micah

Connecticut
Handler – Craig
Nate, Katie, Zion

Iowa
Handler – Ilene
Lock, Brighton Kitana

Florida
Handler – Tony
Alex, Audrey w/parents James & Alice

Person of Interest
Eleanor Anderson/Ellie/Geist

Special Assignment
Harley

Hostile Opposition
Norwegian Special Operations Commando
(Forsvarets Spesialstyrker)

Dear Readers,

I AM HAVING SO MUCH FUN with this series!

In Book II—*Imminence*—our superheroes are commissioned by the FBI to engage in a specific operation. Their ages and super-human abilities make them a unique team for this assignment.

On top of this new commission, the Vikings from Norway are making their first attempt to destroy our heroes' superpowers, and they are proving to be an arduous opponent.

The team's battles will become increasingly more difficult as they gain more experience and further develop their superpowers. This immortal foe is spiraling them further into the paranormal world.

Because my kids and grandkids are the main characters in this series, I am writing their character and dialogue related to their personalities which makes it so fun for me!

I have included information about the characters—it is important not only for this book but for the next six to follow.

I hope you enjoy this series! Thank you for sharing in the journey!

Love, *Debbie*

Immortal

living forever; never dying.
'our mortal bodies are inhabited
by immortal souls.'

PROLOGUE

The strength of a family, like the strength of an army,
is in its loyalty to each other.

RANNUG REMAINED IN THE SHADOWS—watching his progenitors from afar.

Specialized experts in every area of combat and weaponry were brought to Mayajaal to physically prepare the cousins and give them ample time to hone their superhuman powers.

The assignments are coming. Their lives will change drastically, and duties to their country become more demanding. Their extraordinary abilities are pushed to the limit; they will soon realize that loyalty to each other will prove a significant factor in their survival.

The battles will start slow—their first assignment will find them at risk to the notorious Greblos family, whose rivalry with the Nessumsar family stretches back centuries.

They will meet the immortals—those given only one charge—to destroy the Nessumsar family and eradicate their superhuman powers so they can never resurface again.

Would Rannug regret his decision nearly a decade ago? Or would he prove to the Vikings in the old world that his family would be the most successful band of superheroes the world had ever known?

Rannug could only wait and wonder—are they ready?

∾ 1 ∾

WE ARE ALREADY DEAD

"WE KNEW they would migrate here someday."

"They didn't migrate; they were already here."

Young and anxious, Alpo rolled his eyes. "Well, someone came first; that's why they were already here."

The older Viking nodded, "You are correct, but this family grew up in America—they have never lived in Norway or Denmark. It was their great-grandfather who came here first." Sulo laced his fingers and sat back in his chair, deep in thought.

Alpo waited impatiently. He surveyed the others, sitting quietly, waiting for direction from Sulo. He didn't understand why there had to be so much contemplation. *'Let's just take them out!'* He had proposed earlier but was quickly stifled by other council members.

Finally, Sulo stood. "It is necessary to converse with my superiors. Let's not," he turned to Alpo, "To use your words, mess this up."

The rest of the council stood, and Alpo quickly followed suit. He was new here, but he did know what that motion meant.

Sulo immediately began shrinking; once a bat, he shot straight into the sky and, in seconds, was out of sight. The rest of the council quickly morphed and took to the sky behind him, Alpo taking up the rear.

Erikki, one of the younger council members, dropped back next to him. They didn't talk while in bat form, but he conveyed his thoughts to Alpo. *'You needn't worry. In due time there will be more action than you can handle. I promise you that.'*

Alpo shot back, *'They don't want to pursue them. How can we fight them then?'*

Erikki squinted his already beady eyes, *'Because, Alpo, we have an advantage. We are already dead.'*

THESE BATS CAN TALK?!

"WHAT'S WRONG WITH HER?" Harley's eyes widened.

"She's cray, cray—what else is new?" Mack rolled his eyes in his sister's direction. Haydee often messed with them, so he wasn't too concerned about her threat to jump without a chute in defiance of not being chosen to parachute in, but instead to remain in the chopper with the pilot.

It was hard to hear over the helicopter's roar, even with the headsets.

Haydee stood next to the open door. "Look," she yelled, "I have been practicing with Noelle. I've got this!"

Mack and Harley exchanged a quick glance but were distracted when Daverick announced from the pilot's seat, "We're close about ten kilometers out."

Mack's thoughts raced over their mission. 'This is a covert operation; get in, get out, and take what you came for. Don't be a hero; you're not recovering a person. This is a commodity—not worth dying for.'

Mack had stared at the agent until it became uncomfortable. Finally, the agent sighed, 'Just do it. You'll understand later.'

"Haydee, what the…?"

Mack jerked around at Harley's shrill scream to see their sister launch out the open door at twenty-thousand feet. He knew she was falling at a hundred and twenty miles an hour, with no parachute.

Instinctively, Mack and Harley jumped from the open door, attempting to dive fast enough to catch Haydee.

Almost immediately, Haydee realized she had not thoroughly considered her decision to jump. In her excitement, she had forgotten to wait for Noelle's text; now what?

Haydee tried to bring her body into a free fall position, but it wasn't happening. She was spiraling out of control, and she knew it. Maybe her little ploy to trick her brothers was not such a great idea, but with the ground spinning beneath her and no way for her to control her fall, it was too late.

Out of the corner of his eye, Mack saw a figure coming directly at them. She was coming fast, and he knew it was Noelle who could fly. Mack's panicked heartbeat slowed a little.

Noelle zipped past both men directly toward Haydee, who was uncontrollably tumbling toward the ground.

Mack gave Harley a hand signal, and they both pulled their chutes. Knowing Harley would not crash in a heap on the ground, he turned his attention to the drop zone the two were supposed to land on.

Landing within a few feet of their target, Harley scrambled to pull his chute in, simultaneously yelling to anyone who could hear, "I'm going to kill her!"

Mack stuffed his chute in his backpack. "A few minutes ago, you were worrying about her dying."

"Well, she didn't, so now I'm going to take care of it for her."

Mack chuckled, "Relax, bro. Let's get in and get out."

Harley scoffed but followed his bother.

After donning their boots, they ditched their backpacks. To

blend in with the workers on the Cairo site, they wore long-sleeved T-shirts and cargo pants. There were more than a few Caucasians among the native workers, so they should not stand out too much, but to be safe, they both rubbed dirt on their arms and faces before entering the excavation site.

The traces of a 4,500-year-old temple dedicated to the ancient Egyptian sun god, Ra, had recently been uncovered south of Cairo at the site of Abu Ghurab. Mack and Harley had one mission, to gather at least one seal of the pharaohs from the 5th and 6th Dynasties.

The seals had been found on some of the artifacts from the second deposit.

The two crept closer and immediately blended in with the workers. One of the Egyptian excavators looked up from his work, "Is Salam Alaykum."

Harley responded immediately, "WA alaykum is Salam."

The man turned back to his work, and Mack sighed with relief.

Harley had taken quickly to most of the dialects the Nessumsar family had learned the past year and a half, but Mack still needed help with many, and Egyptian was way out of his comfort zone. He would have said "hi" and hoped for the best.

Indiscreetly, Mack pulled out a picture from his pocket and looked at the image they were supposed to locate and the general area it should be. He showed it to Harley, and the two quickly approached what looked like that location.

Meanwhile...

Noelle latched onto Haydee's sleeve, struggling against the weight of her older cousin. It didn't help that Haydee's legs and arms were flailing wildly as she struggled to gain control of her body.

Haydee tried to get hold of Noelle's arm, but the velocity of the wind as they plunged through the air made it more difficult than either girl had imagined.

The ground was rushing up, and Noelle knew she had only two options. Let go of Haydee, which was not an option she was willing to accept or attempt to wrap her arms around Haydee's waist, slow their descent as much as she could, and both hit the ground together.

Noelle threw her body toward Haydee, successfully pulling her into a bear hug, but suddenly another idea. Noelle secured Haydee with one arm around her chest, locking it under her shoulders, and then, in one quick move, she punched her other arm straight into the air. It worked! Both girls shot skyward for several yards allowing Noelle to gain control of her trajectory and slowly bring them to a soft landing.

"I'm flying!" Haydee yelled.

"No, I'm flying—you're just a freeloading passenger!"

Once safely on earth again, both girls burst into laughter.

Noelle collapsed to the ground. "What's wrong with you? You didn't even wait for my text that I was on my way!"

"I knew you would be here." Haydee's eyes widened.

"Yeah, well, I almost didn't make it. I can fly, but not faster than a speeding bullet!" Noelle coined a phrase from Superman.

"The important thing is that we are here—on the ground—alive—not dead."

Noelle leaned back on her elbows and looked up to the cloudless sky. "And how, might I ask, are you going to get back to the chopper, you know, where you are supposed to be?" she cocked her head to one side, "where is that chopper anyway?"

Haydee looked up now, too. "Daverick won't be back until he gets a signal from Mack and Harley after they have the artifact."

Haydee changed the subject, "Can't you fly me?"

Noelle stood and brushed the dirt off her jeans. "No can do. The turbulence is too much for me to get that close to the helicopter. Maybe by myself, but not dragging you along."

"Oh, well, that's not happy news."

Noelle laughed, "Guess we didn't think of that part."

Haydee looked around, "Let's find some shade. We might be

here for a while." She pulled out her cell phone and texted Harley, unsure if he would get it.

I know Mack is mad at me. Maybe you are too. I'm here on the ground with Noelle. I think we're close to where you guys are. Please let me know when the chopper will return to pick you up.

The two girls walked over to a clump of Banyan trees and collapsed in the shade.

"It's hot, and we have no water."

Haydee nodded, acknowledging Noelle's obvious observation.

"I hope we don't get kicked off the team," sighed Noelle.

Haydee took a deep breath, "Me too. After all, we are family, if that counts at all." She suddenly turned to her younger cousin. "I'm sorry, Noelle. I thought it would be fun."

Noelle laughed, "Except for near death, it was!"

They both laughed and laid back in the soft dirt.

Haydee abruptly sat up and sent a text to Daverick in the chopper.

Can you pick us up? Me and Noelle?

Silence.

"Apparently not," Noelle chuckled.

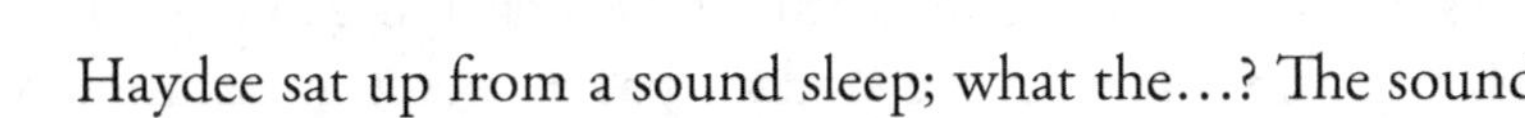

Haydee sat up from a sound sleep; what the...? The sound was like the rapid flapping of wings; blackness closed around her.

"Noelle, Noelle!" she hissed.

"What...?" Noelle brushed her hair out of her eyes. Suddenly she jumped to her feet.

The girls exchanged a panicked look as they backed closer to the trunks of the Banyan trees. They clasped hands, frozen in fear.

The darkness was caused by a thick cloud of bats, hundreds of bats, and they were closing in on them. Some of the smaller ones darted towards the girls coming within inches of their faces but withdrew as quickly as they had come.

'These are two of them…'

Startled, Haydee tried to see whose thoughts she was hearing, but no one was around. Only bats.

'But the main two?'

'There isn't a main two; they are all equally as menacing.'

The bats are talking. Impossible!

"Noelle, these bats can talk!"

Noelle's expression turned to horror, but she said nothing.

The pounding of the bats' wings became deafening, and both girls covered their ears with their hands, but their fate seemed inevitable.

One after another, the bats hit the girls on their heads, chest, and backs. Several darted into their legs, stinging with every blow. Running to escape seemed impossible as they were surrounded, and the impending darkness continued to close in as the bats multiplied.

Noelle tried to fly, but the gale force of the bats wings forced her to the ground.

A loud groan seemed to come from the trees behind them, and the girls spun around only to see the trees lifting out of the ground, their roots cracking sending splinters and leaves spiraling in every direction.

Another loud sound came from behind the bats, and instinctively, they scattered, revealing an enormous bear charging toward them.

"Mack!" screamed Haydee, and at that moment, it occurred to her that Harley was controlling the trees.

Haydee pulled on Noelle's hand, ducking as she ran under the jagged tree roots and away from the bats.

'Retreat!' was all Haydee heard, and in an instant, the bats gathered into a massive black cloud and collectively disappeared into the sky.

Over the roar of the chopper, they heard Daverick's voice through the speaker on Harley's phone.

"What the heck?... I'm comin' round." Maverick called as the sound of the chopper drifted into the distance.

"Nice one, Haydee." Mack morphed back into himself and strode deliberately toward his sister. But he stopped his lecture when she threw herself into his arms.

"Thank you! Thank both of you!" Haydee saw Harley gently lowering the Banyan trees into the gaping hole.

Harley scowled at his sister but chuckled and draped his arm around Noelle's shoulders. "She talked you into this?"

Noelle grimaced. "She didn't have to talk too much. It…it didn't quite work out quite as well as we planned."

࿇ 3 ࿇

GUNNER

LIKE ALWAYS, the mood was energized in the classroom the family had built on Mayajaal. It wasn't a room—more like a bowery—very large and open on three sides.

Benches were added for classroom discussions and instruction but could easily be moved to allow physical training and exercise.

The newest addition had them all in awe. A wall-to-wall, ceiling-to-floor computer screen filled the entire space. In front of the screen, several small computer consoles flanked another console almost double in size. The massive climatized metal cabinet equipped with sliding doors to house the entire system against inclement weather and heat.

Acting on an earlier direction from his Uncle Biorn, Lock pulled a stool up to the larger middle console. He waved his hand just above it, and the buttons began whirring as the panel of lights lit up. Several images flashed on the screen.

Everyone crowded closer to get a better look.

"What's this all about?" Spencer asked what everyone else was thinking.

"We have someone we want you to meet," Biorn spoke from the back of the group but went to the front. He stopped when he was next to Lock.

Biorn was followed by a tall, stocky, dark-haired man with a neatly trimmed beard and mustache. His blue eyes sparkled when he turned to face the group.

"This is Gunner."

The man grinned and half saluted. He silently observed the group, making it a point to look into each of their faces.

Katie leaned close to her sister's ear, "He's kinda hot."

Kitana shook her head and laughed. "You think every guy is hot," she whispered.

"Shh."

They both looked behind and scowled at Nate. His arms folded; he didn't even glance at them. His gaze remained fixed on Gunner.

"Why are you here?" without waiting for an answer, Aubrey craned her neck to see where her parents, uncles, and aunts were standing in a group. She pointed in their direction. "My dad's over there."

Gunner smiled at nine-year-old Aubrey, "And so he is." He nodded in James's direction.

Tiago, who had remained quiet until now, said, "Your dad will always be here, Aubrey." He turned to the group, "Gunner is your new Team Leader. He and I served in the Navy for a while. I left for civilian life, and after he finished out his service, Gunner went on to be a part of NCSI." He acknowledged the newcomer again, "Special Agent Mont Gunderson."

Gunner nodded at the group, "Just Gunner. I'm looking forward to working with all of you."

Alex grinned and nodded his approval. "The dream teams?"

Gunner grinned at twelve-year-old Alex, "Sounds good to me."

Gunner glanced at Tiago, but then his smile faded. The entire team noticed and gave him their full attention. Even Aubrey.

Gunner began, "All of you have been on some training missions, and most of you came through with flying colors." He turned and nodded at Lock, who pushed some buttons on the console.

The image changed from several scenes to one video that filled the entire screen.

Audible gasps and some chuckle swept through the team as Haydee's out-of-control skydive suddenly appeared.

Haydee covered her face with her hands but then looked at the group through her spread fingers. She was visibly embarrassed.

Appearing mortified, Noelle quickly scanned everyone's faces, finally landing on Haydee. Her eyes widened.

Gunner waved his hand at the screen, and the image froze. He jutted his thumb behind him but didn't take his eyes off the team. "This," he began, "could have been a disaster. I'm not going to dwell on it because it came out okay. In the future, stick to your own superpower."

"But I…"

Gunner held up his hand to stop Haydee. He looked at her, "I know you were not trying to use it; you depended on Noelle. Don't do that again."

Haydee exchanged a quick glance with Noelle, who looked relieved.

Gunner shook his head, "Big mistake, girls."

"I'll say," Mack rolled his eyes.

Gunner glanced in Mack's direction but said nothing.

He turned his attention back to the screen, and Lock scanned through more images.

Everyone gasped as the image on the screen froze briefly, a video filled with hundreds of screeching bats, then just as quickly, the screen turned to static.

The room fell silent except for the loud static.

Gunner waved at the screen again, and the static stopped. "We've been monitoring you through these initial test missions."

Brooke raised her hand, "But some of us have already completed missions with the FBI."

"Or the CIA," added Spencer.

Gunner nodded, "That's true. But things are changing. With some handlers, we think you can work independently. Obviously, your abilities are way above the average human's."

"Handlers?" asked Micah.

All heads nodded in agreement with Micah's question, but then Spencer said, "Most of the information…"

"Intelligence…"

Spencer acknowledged Gunnar, "Yes, intelligence. They kind of go ahead of us and get as much information as they can for us to do our job," he nodded at Gunner.

"Spencer is right on track; some of you have worked with handlers. You'll meet my team later; they will work with you and your handlers."

"Our new concern is these bats—they were a complete surprise. What you see on this screen is the last thing we see.

He looked directly at Haydee, Noelle, Harley, and Mack. "I want to meet with you, you, you, and you.

I know there are a lot of questions, probably the same questions I have, but let's hold off on those for a day or so. Right now, you have company."

He motioned to their trainers, who had just arrived.

"Get your gear; it's all combat today."

Most met the announcement enthusiastically, but there were also a few collective sighs.

"Dang it," Micah whispered to Noelle, "I want to know more about the bats now."

Noelle gave her a faint smile, but it was apparent she was nervous, and she hurried to catch up with Mack, Haydee, and Harley, who were all walking with Gunner toward their parents.

Richard noticed them, too; he took Amanda's hand, and they joined Tiago and Brooke.

Brighton ran toward Ava and Zion, who were talking to Katie and Kitana.

"Can you guys believe those bats? What do you think they mean?" Brighton tried to whisper, but that was not her strong suit.

"Beats me, but they're kind of cool," said Zion.

"What? Cool?" Ava looked mortified. "What could be cool about hundreds of bats flying at you? You're so weird, Zion."

"He's a guy," laughed Kitana.

"That explains it," Katie agreed with her sister.

"You two don't have a brother, though. Brothers are different than guys."

Zion rolled his eyes at his sister while scowling, "Oh, okay."

"This is a reality we may all have to deal with." Spencer joined Brighton, Kitana, and Katie.

Zion's eyes widened, "The bats?"

Spencer shrugged, "Maybe."

❧ 4 ☙

UNEXPECTED CHANGES

"SENIOR AIRMAN NEITSNIBUR?"

"Yes, Sir." Grant stood at attention and saluted. He had no idea why he had been called into his Captain's quarters this morning, and he was even more surprised to see Lieutenant Colonel Rothers.

Grant glanced around, "Captain Rodriguez, Sir."

Captain Rodriguez smiled briefly, then motioned to a chair next to the Lieutenant.

Grant saluted the Lieutenant Colonel but stood at attention.

"At ease, Neitsnibur. Take a seat."

Grant quickly obeyed, but it didn't dispel his anxiety. He chose not to look at the Lieutenant.

"Lieutenant Colonel Rothers," he extended his hand to Grant.

"Sir," Grant hesitated, then shook his hand. His mind was racing, trying to think of anything serious enough to get him discharged from the Airforce. Just a few months away from promotion to Staff Sergeant, this meeting did not seem like a step in that direction.

Captain Rodriguez, not known for his congenial mannerisms, seemed unusually friendly today, leaving Grant even more confused.

"No doubt you're wondering what we called you in for."

"Yes, Sir."

The Captain continued, "I still can't believe this, and nothing against you, Airman Neitsnebur; this is just so out of the ordinary," he chuckled and continued, "Mind you, the Lieutenant General, a three-star general, has requested you be immediately promoted to Master Sergeant."

Grant's eyes widened, and he could not hold back the gasp that escaped his throat. "Sir?"

Captain Rodriguez and Lieutenant Colonel Rothers exchanged a quick glance, and both chuckled.

"Sir, why?"

Lieutenant Colonel Rothers looked directly at Grant, "Classified."

"Sir?"

Captain Rodriguez had been resting his elbows on his desk; now, he leaned back in his chair. "Exactly, classified. We know nothing more than that."

"But shouldn't you, or aren't you supposed to know? Sir?"

The Lieutenant nodded, "One would think. But these orders come from the top. You are being transferred to Nellis, at least for now."

"The time being..."

"Airman Neitsnibur, that's all the information we have." The Captain glanced at the Lieutenant.

Lieutenant Colonel Rothers nodded, "Apparently, you're stopping in Belize?"

Grant's eyes widened, "Okay…"

"Any idea why, Airman?"

Grant looked directly at the Lieutenant. His sister, brother, and cousins had been sworn to complete secrecy about the family island of Mayajaal in Belize. He shook his head, "No Sir, uh, Sirs."

Captain Rodriguez stood but he did not look convinced. Lieutenant Colonel Rothers stood as well, and Grant jumped to his feet.

"It's been a pleasure working with you, Son. We wish you the best."

Grant stood at attention and saluted both the Captain and the Lieutenant. "Thank you."

They both shook his hand.

"Dismissed."

Grant turned on his heel and walked briskly to the door.

"Airman?"

Grant turned around, Sir?"

"Pack your gear; you're being picked up by private jet at 1800 hours," said Captain Rodriguez.

Grant nodded, "Sir."

"And Airman."

Grant looked at Lieutenant Colonel Rothers, "Sir?"

"Top secret, say nothing to anyone. That means no one."

"Okay. Sir."

Grant's heart was racing so fast he could almost hear it, and once in the hall, he stumbled back against the wall. His head was spinning. He glanced at his watch. 1500 hours.

I should call Mom.

He thought again, no, she probably already knows. Besides, tell no one.

Grant scanned Travis Air Force Base three hours later until the plane rose above the clouds. The only passenger on the plane except for the pilot and a man identifying himself only as Damion, he sat back in his seat. They both seemed nice enough, but they didn't say much.

Grant settled back for the flight to Mayajaal.

What is happening right now?

∽ 5 ∽

LEAVING

SAMUAL NESSUMSAR stood in the hanger bay of the USS Carl Vinson somewhere in the Pacific Ocean. He had his camera set to take pictures of the F-35C Lightening II Fighter jets when they took off from one of the neighboring carriers.

A Seaman Recruit, he would never get tired of this. The sound of the jets taking off was almost deafening—they left one after another for a regular training run, and Samual snapped pictures and short videos. The sound of the jet engines always took his breath away.

"Hey, Nessumsar."

Samual turned to see Petty Officer Jewkes walking towards him. He didn't wait for Samual to answer. "You're wanted - uh, Captains Stateroom."

"For what?"

"How should I know? Just delivering the message."

"Okay, on my way."

Petty Office Jewkes nodded, then turned and disappeared behind a plane.

Samual put his cell phone in his pocket. He stopped for a second, looking across the ocean.

What's this all about?

Samual climbed up the first of several steep ladders, his mind swirling with all the possibilities he could be called to the Captain's quarters.

This has never happened to me before.

The knot in the pit of Samual's stomach grew with each step he took. He was sweating profusely when he reached the Captain's quarters. He darted into the closest head to wipe the sweat off his face and neck. But then he splashed water on his face, grabbed some paper towels, and wiped his forehead.

He took a deep breath, stepped before the Captain's door, and gave two quick knocks.

The door opened, and Samual came face to face with Quarter Master Dickson, who moved out of the way so Samual could enter.

Seated behind his desk, Captain McGee looked up. Samual stood at attention and saluted. "Sir."

"At ease, Nessumsar." The Captain motioned to the chair on the other side of the desk, "Take a seat."

Samual glanced at the quartermaster, who remained standing near the door.

Seriously, I'm not going to try to escape.

Captain McGee got straight to the point. "We have orders to advance you and ship you back to Coronado."

Samual sat straight up in his chair. "Sir? I—I don't understand."

The Captain shook his head, "Neither do I. But I have my orders. You'll leave here as Lieutenant, Junior Grade. This is an honorary promotion but is required."

"Required for what, Sir?"

Samual's surprised look made the Captain chuckle. "You know as much as I do. I'm just following orders from Rear Admiral Jones."

"Rear Admiral, Sir? Why would he…?"

Captain McGee shook his head. "You got me, Nessumsar."

The Captain shuffled through some papers on his desk, found what he was looking for, and read, "You leave here at 600 hours tomorrow morning—brief stop in Hawaii, then apparently onto Belize?"

Captain McGee looked up, "Any idea what that's all about?"

Samual swallowed hard, "No, no, Sir."

The Captain looked directly at Samual but said nothing. Without taking his eyes from him, Captain McGee pushed a folder and a pen across the desk. Samual signed in the two designated spots and pushed them back.

"You've been a good Seaman, Nessumsar; exceptional. I wish you the best. Maybe you might come back here after whatever you're doing is over. You were hoping to go on to SWICC, right?"

Samual nodded, "Yes, Sir."

Captain McGee stood and extended his hand to Samual.

Samual jumped to his feet and shook the Captain's hand vigorously. "Sir, thank you, Sir."

"Thank you, *Lieutenant* Nessumsar; good luck." Captain McGee grinned.

Samual saluted, turned, and exited the stateroom. The quartermaster closed the door behind him.

Samual took a huge breath.

Now what?

ASSIGNMENTS

LOCK'S SUPERPOWER was a shapeshifter. The easiest thing he morphed into was a Ninja Turtle, but he had been practicing other shapes. The training for that was brutal, so in many ways, he was glad that today the Ninja Turtle, if needed, was perfect. This assignment also included Kitana, who could become invisible, and Brighton, who could not only fly but could immediately summon extraordinary strength. She and her brother, Spencer, both had that same ability.

All three had been assigned one handler for this mission and would there when the plane landed.

"Do we know where we're going?"

Kitana took a window seat on the Nessumsar private jet.

Shane leaned around from the pilot seat, "I know," he chuckled.

"I guess he's the one who needs to know." Lock sat across from Kitana, and Brighton sat beside him.

"This is so different; we usually are assisting agents, but now we're alone," Brighton's voice trailed off. "Not sure I like that idea."

"Ya, me either," agreed Kitana.

"Oh, don't worry, it will be fine." Lock didn't sound too convinced, but he laughed.

Both girls jumped when Lock suddenly became a Ninja turtle.

"Lock?" whined Kitana.

Lock was himself again, "Dang it, I wasn't actually going for that."

Kitana rolled her eyes and glanced at Brighton, who was chuckling.

Kitana gave her an irritated look.

"Sorry! I think it's funny."

The plane taxied down the short runway, and soon, the tiny island of Mayajaal was a dot in the distance.

"Hey, Lock, wake up. We'll be landing in about half an hour." Brighton shook her cousin's shoulder.

Lock sat up and rubbed his eyes. "Landing where?"

Kitana plopped down across from Lock and Brighton, "Iowa." She said flatly, "I wonder what could be so important here."

"People are just as important everywhere; it doesn't matter where they live, Kitana," said Brighton.

"I know that I'm talking about scenery, not people."

Brighton and Lock laughed, "The state is beautiful in its own way," said Lock, "Miles of corn fields and farmland. I rode with my dad through Iowa once on a run he took to the east coast."

"That's cool," said Brighton, "I wasn't being negative. I was thinking of corn, not corn fields."

"Seatbelts on kids." Shane's voice came over the speakers.

Thirty minutes later, the three kids stepped off the plane and were met by a woman who appeared to be in her early thirties.

She greeted them with a faint smile, shook all their hands, and said her name was Ilene. She took them through the tiny airport to a black SUV beside the curb.

Ilene explained, "We have a hotel suite for you," she turned to Lock, "It has two bedrooms. I need you to stay in your rooms until we meet for breakfast in the morning. We'll eat in your suite."

"Do we know yet what we're doing?" asked Kitana.

"You'll know in the morning. But I can tell you it involves school," said Ilene.

"School?"

Ilene laughed when they all chorused the word.

"Yes, but it won't be like regular school. I'll explain in the morning."

The three sighed.

Once inside the hotel suite, Ilene instructed them to stay in the room and stay together.

"That's it? That's all we get?"

Ilene smiled at Lock, nodded briefly, and walked out of the room.

"Night," she called

Daverick was already in the helicopter when Micah, Spencer, Mack, and Ava climbed aboard.

"Buckle up! We need to get going."

The four stowed their backpacks, pulled on their headsets, and clamored into their seats.

"We're going to California, right?" asked Mack.

"Yes, Northern California, though, not LA."

"Dang it."

"You just got back from there," said Ava, "Why so anxious to go back?"

"Wanted to see my dog; I'm starting to think keeping him may not be a good idea."

"Why can't you bring him here?" asked Spencer.

"I brought it up but was told for now that I can't. I'm not sure why."

"Maybe because we're not here all the time?" `

Mack sighed, "Yeah, you're probably right, Micah, and I'm not always home either."

Everyone was quiet. Mack's somber mood put a damper on everything, and they all sat in silence except for the whir of the copter engines.

After several minutes, Ava said, "So, do we know what we're doing when we get there?"

Mack looked away from the window and grinned, "I'm okay, by the way, sorry."

Ava sat beside Mack, putting her hand on his shoulder, "I'm sure we'll figure out—the dog and stuff."

Mack laughed, "Yeah, I'm sure we will. Anyway, we're meeting our handler, right?"

"I think we each have our own handler?"

Micah shrugged, "I don't think so, but I really have no idea." She looked at the other three, who appeared to be just as clueless.

Daverick landed the helicopter at the Philip S. W. Goldson Airport, where a private jet awaited the four.

They said their goodbyes to Daverick, exited the helicopter, and boarded the plane.

"I would have liked to go to the bathroom." Micah buckled her seat belt and looked at her cousins. She sighed, "I know, I know, there's a bathroom on the plane." She grimaced, "I hate airplane bathrooms. They're so—tiny."

"A little claustrophobic, maybe?" asked Spencer.

Micah sighed again, "A lot, actually."

"We'll keep that in mind." Mack ruffled her hair, and Micah pulled away. When the plane reached cruising altitude, she unbuckled her seat belt and headed toward the back of the aircraft.

Her three cousins fell asleep, but Micah was too restless. She sat back and turned to look out the window at the cloudless sky.

Something caught her eye. She sat up and leaned closer to the window. It seemed to be a black cloud coming right toward the plane.

Birds?

But the cloud was now right outside the window.

"Bats!" Micah screamed and jumped to her feet, startling the others from their sleep.

Mack looked out the window but saw nothing. "Where were they, Micah?"

She pointed to the window, "Right there. I thought they were birds at first."

Mack sighed, "We had bats attack us in Egypt, but why here?"

"That's what Gunner was telling us about?" asked Ava.

Mack nodded.

"The better question is, what are they doing at this altitude?"

"Yeah, that's a little weird," said Spencer. "You're sure they were bats?"

Micah nodded vigorously. "Absolutely sure."

Spencer and Ava exchanged a puzzled look, but Mack was texting. He put his phone back in his pocket and looked at the other three.

"I texted Gunner. Figured we should at least let him know about the bats."

They all looked out the window seeing only clouds, but the uneasy feeling hung in the air.

Five hours later, the plane touched down in San Jose, California. When the four cousins exited the stairs, they were met by a woman who appeared to be in her late forties. She flashed a badge at them, introduced herself as Char, and motioned for them to follow her to a waiting black SUV.

Once seated, they all exchanged puzzled looks.

Char sat quietly in the front passenger seat.

The driver, a young African American man, was much more jovial. "How are we today?" He looked at them through the rearview mirror.

The cousins relaxed, and Mack answered, "We're good." He glanced at the other three, "I think."

"Yeah," laughed Spencer, "We're super."

Ava added, "Just wondering what we're doing."

"You'll know soon enough. I'm Henry, and I'll be your driver while you're in San Jose." He glanced at Char, "She'll be here too; she is just a little more on the quiet side."

Char glanced at Henry, but her demeanor remained the same.

They drove for about twenty minutes before Henry pulled the SUV to a stop in front of an old two-story home. The entire street was lined with similar two-story, older homes. It seemed like a quiet neighborhood.

Without shutting off the engine, Henry turned around in his seat, "I will always pick you up, but it may not be in this exact vehicle. We often change that up for security purposes.

The cousins gathered their backpacks and exited the vehicle. Char left, too, and met them on the driver's side.

The look on her face was an annoyance. She slung a large bag over her shoulder, "Look, I'm not excited about working with a bunch of kids. Let's just start there. I have a real problem with your supposedly *special powers*, so let's just make sure you obey orders, get this job done, and get you back to your private little fantasy island, wherever that is."

Not one to be pushed around, Mack immediately said, "I'm hardly a kid; I'm twenty-eight."

Char rolled her eyes, "Like I said."

Henry had his window down and shook his head, "Lighten up, Char."

She scoffed, turned on her heel, and started up the sidewalk toward the house's front door.

The cousins all glanced at Henry.

He smiled, "Her bark is worse than her bite."

"My bite is worse," snapped Mack staring after Char.

That made his cousins laugh.

"*That* is so true," said Ava.

Henry chuckled, "Not sure what that means, but I'll see you kids, uh adults," he grinned at Mack, "Later."

Mack laughed, "Yeah, okay. Thanks, Henry."

Henry pulled away from the curve with a quick wave, and they all joined Char on the front porch.

She handed Mack a cell phone. "This is a burner phone; you'll use it to contact me and whatever other contacts you're given when you go inside."

They all nodded but said nothing.

Mack took the phone, stuck it in a side pocket of his backpack, and zipped it shut. He looked at Char, his expression defiant.

Char glared at him, "Don't mess with me."

Mack started to say something, but Spencer grabbed his arm.

Char opened the front door. She turned back to the four, "Wait here." She disappeared inside and shut the door behind her.

"I don't like her."

Micah rolled her eyes at Mack, "Oh really, we didn't notice.'

Spencer said, "Look, man, we just need to get the job done, whatever that means. Don't let her get under your skin. She's like fifty, so to her, we probably are kids."

Mack scowled, "I guess so."

"I know so." Spencer half smiled, but he was serious and continued, "We don't even know what we're doing here."

The door opened, and Char motioned for them to come inside.

When they did, they were all shocked at what they saw.

Expecting furniture, maybe a fireplace like any other house, it was nothing of the sort.

Instead, computer stations and desks. There seemed to be only one big room on the main floor, and at each station, men and women were intently engaged in what was happening on their screens.

What appeared to be windows outside the house were covered on the inside. Walls had been built over the windows. They were no overhead lights, only desk lamps at each computer.

They followed Char through the neatly organized desks to the far back wall.

She stopped in front of a desk where the computer had three screens. The man at the desk had flaming red hair and wore black-rimmed glasses.

Char stood next to him, "Meet Frank. You'll be working with him," she motioned to Mack's backpack, "His number is in that phone."

Mack nodded, and Char continued, "Frank, this is Mack, Spencer, Ava, and Micah."

Frank spun around on his stool. "Pleased." His face lit up, "Can't wait to see your superpowers."

It was difficult to tell if he was being serious or sarcastic.

Char shook her head and rolled her eyes, "Just get the job done." She faced the cousins, "I'll be back," with that, she walked away and jogged up a long staircase.

"Wow, just like the Terminator," said Ava.

"She probably is a terminator," Micah chuckled.

"At least related," scoffed Spencer.

Frank turned back to his computer, "At least first cousins."

No one was sure how to react to Frank's comment about Char, but then he laughed.

A collective sigh escaped all of them.

Frank enlarged an image on one of the screens, and they all gathered closer.

"This mission, if you choose to accept it, is your assignment." Frank chuckled, "I've always wanted to say that."

Mack laughed, "Will the phone self-destruct?"

Frank gave him a side glance, "Anything's possible."

Mack's eyebrows shot up, "Seriously?"

But they were all distracted by the image on the screen. An attractive woman with short, cropped hair. Slim built and wearing black jeans, a white blouse with loose-fitting long sleeves, and a black vest open in the front. The starfish tattoo on the left side of her neck was easy to see.

Frank put the cursor on her face, "This is our subject."

Mack squirmed, "I know her, not well, but she played with Haydee on San Jose's soccer team."

Frank looked directly at Mack, "Exactly. Nothing we do is by accident."

"What did she do?" asked Ava.

"Not did, doing. She is the mastermind of a string of robberies. We've been watching her for a while now, but she has jumped to a whole new level."

"What do you mean?" asked Spencer.

Frank turned to a different screen and enlarged the image.

Spencer leaned in closer, "Looks like a high school hallway."

"It is." Frank turned to face the cousins. "She has connections all over the US, and now she is enlisting high school kids in illegal activities."

"So, what do you want us to do?" asked Mack.

Frank's face suddenly became serious, "Stop her."

❧ 7 ❧

QUESTIONS

TIAGO AND BROOK YELLEK sat across from Gunner, who was going through the notes he had taken from his meeting with Mack, Haydee, and Harley.

Noelle's parents, Richard, and Amanda Nessumsar, sat on the two chairs next to Tiago.

Tiago asked, "The kids seemed alarmed by the bats but not threatened. Should they be?"

Gunner scratched his chin, "I have no idea. From all accounts, your kids told me it seems like a random attack on two unsuspecting girls. I tried to find some information on bats in Cairo, and all I could come up with are fruit bats and something called Palearctic Bats; both species are small."

Richard moved closer to the screen, "They look like bats I've seen in California. He scrolled through his phone, then held it out for the others to see, "That's a western Mastiff Bat."

Brooke pulled the same image up on her phone. She studied it and then looked at the commuter screen. "But the bats that attacked Noelle and Haydee were bigger, weren't they?"

Amanda pointed to the screen, "Seems so. Ugh, they are so ugly."

Gunner sighed. "I guess we'll find out." He stood, "Thanks for coming. We'll talk more later, but I have some things I need to check on. See you tonight at the info meeting.'

Gunner left, and the four parents sat silently for a few seconds.

"He does end abruptly, doesn't he?" said Brooke.

"He's not much for small talk," said Richard. "Does Gunner know how our kids got their superpowers?"

Tiago's eyes widened, "I would think so."

"What if he doesn't?" asked Brooke.

"Well, he knows they have them. Surely, he would have been filled in." Amanda looked at Richard, "Right?"

Tiago responded, "I don't know. Guess we'll find out tonight.'

⁂

The five sets of parents and single mom Janae gathered in Biorn and Aiko's bungalow.

Aiko piled a plate of sandwiches on the table, and Janae followed her with water and soda. Both women collapsed into chairs.

"This has been a crazy ride the last month," said Biorn. He looked at each of his siblings and their spouses, then picked up a folder from the side table. He moved the sandwiches out of the way and placed the folder on the table.

Referring to the folder, James asked, "Are these the kids' missions? Excluding my kids, of course." He looked at Alice. "I think they're ready for—simple stuff—is there simple stuff?"

Biorn laughed, "Actually…" he handed them stapled papers.

"I do have a question," Emmett searched their faces.

"What's wrong, Emmett?" Biron turned to his brother-in-law.

"I was wondering where Gunner came from. Was he vetted? He's working closely with our kids. I mean, every one of the trainers, pilots, even the cleaning and ground crew you hired, or at least with some of our help. Where did he come from?"

"Good question. He will be here in about half an hour to give us information, in fact, all the information," said Biron.

"But who referred him?" Emmett was not letting up.

"He was sent to us by the director of the CIA. Like you said, we need someone to vet the missions the kids are involved in, and remember, most of them have already worked with the CIA and the FBI."

Emmett nodded but said, "I don't know why, but I have a bad feeling about…I'm not sure what, maybe the bats."

Tatiana scrunched her face, "The bats? Aren't they just bats?"

Emmett shrugged, "I don't know. Was the crow just a crow?"

Everyone chuckled, and Biorn said, "Point taken. But seriously, he came recommended from the top."

He referred them to the second page of the paperwork and began reading:

"Special Agent Mont Gunderson—I'll paraphrase most of this; you guys can get into the details later if you want. But to begin with, he's part of the CIA's covert paramilitary operations unit, Specialist Activities Division (SAD). They are one of America's most secretive and lowest profile special ops organizations."

"Graduating with a 4.20, mind you, from the University of Maryland—College Park. He has computer science, criminal justice, and political science degrees and is trained in every kind of weapon and martial arts on the planet. He also ranks among the top five agents in the highest level of physical fitness."

"Is he married?"

They all laughed at Janae's question.

Her eyes widened, "What? Just asking."

"No, he isn't, but how old are you?"

Janae scowled, "Forty-four, why?"

"Gunner is thirty-eight. So there ya go."

Janae scowled, "Whatever, Biorn."

"Uh, Gunner also speaks fluent Arabic, Chinese, Spanish, and Portuguese, to name a few. He has specialized training in cybersecurity and information technology." Amanda waved the papers in the air. "Okay then…"

"Maybe an older brother?" Janae laughed.

"I have an older brother, a beautiful wife, and four kids; they live in Maryland."

They all looked up.

Gunner pushed the door open with his foot and walked in carrying a box.

Tatiana chuckled, and Janae smacked her on the leg.

"Need some help with that?" Richard stood and took the box from Gunner.

"Thanks, man; I have one more in the jeep."

Gunner disappeared out the door and returned minutes later with another box and an armful of folders.

Biorn grabbed a chair from the bar as Gunner passed the folders to each kid's parents. When he sat down, he noticed the open folder with his name on it on the table before Biorn.

"I see you already have my credentials. Any questions?"

"It's obvious you come highly recommended," said Tiago, "We appreciate you taking the assignment." He paused for a second, "I'm curious, though, why would you leave your job that was highly top secret to come here and work with our kids."

"Good question, Emmett." Gunner sat forward in his chair. "I was selected, but I did have the opportunity to turn it down."

"But you didn't," said James.

"Absolutely not. How often do we get to work with real-life superheroes?" He sat back, rested his elbows on the chair arms, and laced his fingers together. "To be honest, I couldn't believe it was for real. I didn't work on any of the older kids' assignments with the CIA; I was overseas that first year."

The door opened, and Dede walked in.

"Hey, Mom, you made it." Biorn stood and hugged his mom, then she sat next to Janae.

"Barely. The plane was late getting into Belize. I felt bad keeping Shane waiting."

"We would have sent Shane to Arizona to pick you up, Mom, but he was delivering some of the kids to San Jose, and then he took Dalbir to Tabacco Caye to see his family for a couple of days."

"It's fine! I made it didn't I?" Dede turned to Gunner, "You must be the new guy."

"Sorry, Mom, this is Special Agent Mont Gunderson," said Biorn.

"Gunner," he extended his hand, and Dede shook it. "Nice to meet you, ma'am. You're the boss of this group?"

Dede laughed, "Hardly; they kept this whole thing from me for a year." She looked around at her kids, "And now here we are."

"Here we are," echoed Brooke.

"Where are the kids?" asked Dede.

"Let's see, four are in California, and three are in…" Tiago looked at Gunner, "Where are Lock, Kitana, and Brighton?"

"Iowa," said Gunner.

"Iowa?" it was collective from almost the entire group.

Gunner nodded; he referred to the folders, "Let's go through a couple of things. I'd like to review the superpowers first if that's okay with everyone?"

No one objected, and they opened their folders.

"This information will give you an idea of what kind of cases your kids will be involved in. But for the most part, they will be kept out of danger. Those over twenty-five will most likely be assigned to more challenging missions."

Tiago and Brooke exchanged a quick glance.

Gunner noticed that and said, "Your kids are the ones who are over twenty-five?"

Tiago nodded.

"Not until they're ready," Gunner reassured them.

Brooke's sigh was audible.

Gunner looked down at the folders but then abruptly looked up, "I have a better idea; why don't you tell me about your kids. I would like to hear from all of you."

"Do you want to start, James," said Biorn.

James nodded, "Sure. Alex can have fun faster than I can believe, and Audrey can move things with her mind."

Alice added, "It's getting easier to deal with once we convinced Audrey she couldn't move toys into the shopping cart."

That made everyone laugh.

"She is only eight," said Janae, "That's tempting! It would be for me, and I'm forty-four, as I was reminded earlier." She glared at her brother, then said, "Guess I'm next; my youngest, Zeke, is a fast runner like Alex; Ava can make things appear, Grant can hear others' thoughts, and he can also put thoughts into people's minds. It's all so crazy."

Richard picked it up next, "My oldest, Nate, can be invisible but also appear as a Viking. Samual can hear others' thoughts, total telepathic. Lock can become a Ninja Turtle; he's trying to learn to morph into other shapes. Noelle can fly; I'm jealous of that," he chuckled. "Micah is a shapeshifter like Lock; cats and a princess are easy, but she's working on other shapes, same as Lock."

Tatiana said, "Me next? Our girls, Katie, and Kitana, can both become invisible."

"The kids got their superpowers almost eight years ago," said Emmett, "But they had to learn how to use them."

"More like controlling them," agreed Tatiana.

Biorn nodded in agreement, "That's Spencer's too; he can disappear, as he likes to say, and he has incredible strength. Brighton can fly, and the strength thing, too. At times, she's stronger than I am."

Gunner raised his eyebrows, "Seriously?"

Biorn chuckled, "I'm not kidding."

Brooke said, "Mack is a shapeshifter, a bear, but working on other shapes. Haydee can hear other's thoughts, and Harley can control the elements," she shook her head, "If someone were listening right now, they would think we have lost our minds."

They all laughed.

Gunner turned to Dede, "What about Mom? What's your superpower??"

Dede shook her head, "I'm just Mom and Grandma, no superpowers. My ancestor gave those to my grandkids. They have been in my family in Norway for centuries. It's part of our legacy. I had to get out of their way, not try to protect them anymore."

"Yeah, we have Mom to thank for not having our own superpowers," James grinned at his mother.

Dede shrugged, "Sorry, but I obviously didn't do that good of a job. My great-grandfather found them anyway."

"Mom sees spirits," said Tatiana.

"And talks to them," added Brooke.

"That was random," Janae started to laugh.

Gunner raised his eyebrows a second time, "And you don't consider that a superpower?"

Dede smiled, "No, not a superpower."

Gunner's look became more intense, and he waited for Dede to respond.

"It's a gift."

❦ 8 ❦

MORE ASSIGNMENTS

WHEN THE YACHT docked in the Cedar Island Marina, Katie, Nate, and Zion stood on the deck.

"What are we doing in Connecticut?" asked Nate.

Craig, the man who had been traveling with them since they left Belize, stepped up next to Nate. "This is where your assignment is."

Zion and Katie moved over next to them, and Zion asked, "At the beach? Cool."

"Not exactly at the beach, at a high school nearby."

"How close?"

"Morgan High, just a couple of miles inland." Craig turned to Zion, "Close enough?"

"That'll do." Zion pulled his ball cap almost over his eyes, folded his arms, and grinned.

Katie asked, "So, do we know what we're doing?"

"You will soon enough."

The deckhands tied the boat down, and another dropped the steps into place.

The three cousins followed Craig down the steps, along the boardwalk, and to an SUV in VIP parking right next to the dock.

Once inside, Craig said, "When you get to your hotel, Katie will be issued a burner cell, and you will use it for communicating with me throughout the mission. Your cell phones will be disabled."

Nate scowled, "Seriously? And why does Katie have the phone?"

Craig chuckled, "Yes, seriously, on the phones—it's for your own protection, trust me. As far as the burner, it's by age right now." He half smiled, "And apparently, she has about four months on you."

"Wow," Nate scoffed, and Zion laughed.

"You can have the phone, Nate," said Katie.

Nate rolled his eyes. "No, it's fine."

"Yes, it is that phone is assigned to you, Katie, and no one else." Craig looked at all three of them, "And did I mention that the three of you stayed together the entire time. Don't separate for any reason."

Now Katie scowled, "What if I need to go the bathroom? Do they come with me?"

"Not to worry, we got you covered." Craig reached into his backpack and pulled out the burner phone. He placed it in Katie's hand. "My number is programmed—contact one."

Katie looked at the screen, "And the other contact? The 000?"

"That is like 911, but you always try me first. You push that contact if you don't get me after ten minutes. The voice on the other end will help you."

"Uh, why wouldn't you answer?" Zion asked.

"Probably won't happen, just a precaution."

The car stopped, and a man opened the side door of the SUV. Craig climbed out, and the three joined him on the sidewalk before a two-story bed and breakfast. A bell boy nearby started to walk toward them with a baggage cart but stopped when he seemed to notice each of the four only carried backpacks.

Craig handed the bellboy a twenty-dollar bill. He thanked Craig and pushed the cart toward a taxi that had just pulled up behind the SUV.

They followed Craig into the lobby, where he checked them in, and they rode the elevator to their rooms. He opened Katie's room first.

"Oh my gosh, what an adorable room!" Katie squealed, and Craig handed her the key. She hurried inside.

Nate and Zion looked at each other and laughed.

Craig walked past the next door, pointed to it, and said, "My room."

"You're staying here too?"

Craig answered Nate, "Yes," and handed him the key to the third door.

"Katie?"

She laughed and was suddenly right next to Craig.

"Whoa!" Craig jumped and backed away.

"Don't harass the guy so soon." Mack snickered.

"What the…" Craig still stared at Katie.

"That's her superpower," said Zion.

"Yeah, I knew that just—just haven't ever witnessed it."

"I thought we were supposed to stay together," Katie laughed, "I'm sorry, I couldn't resist."

Craig sighed, "Okay, that's actually very cool, a little freaky but still cool."

He eyed all three of them suspiciously, "Anything else—you want to show me?"

"Not right now, boss."

Craig scoffed, "Whatever. So, to continue where I left off… where did I leave off? When you leave these rooms, you are like three peas in a pod."

Katie nodded and got it. She held the phone in her hand, "But if I…"

"Covered," said Craig. He motioned for Nate to open the door to his and Zion's room, and Craig walked directly to the hotel phone on the desk. He pointed to a yellow button. "See that? It calls directly to my cell. Try it."

Zion pushed the button, and Craig's phone rang.

"See, I'm right here. You need me; just push that button. We'll meet in the hall at 7:30 am sharp tomorrow and eat breakfast here. I'll have your orders in the morning."

He scanned their faces, then looked at his watch, "Questions?"

No one responded.

"I took the liberty of ordering dinner, hamburgers, and that stuff from the little sandwich joint next door. It's nearly six, we've been traveling all day, and we've lost two hours. Get some rest. See you in the morning."

"Thanks, man," said Nate, shaking Craig's extended hand.

"Yeah, thanks," said Zion.

"My room is still the coolest," Katie laughed and walked into her room.

"They are exactly the same," Zion rolled his eyes.

She poked her head back out in the hall, "Nope! I have a king; you have two queens! Ha!"

James, Alice, Alex, and Audrey walked up the jet bridge into the Orlando International Airport.

"Isn't Disneyworld close by?" Alex asked his dad.

"Yes, close by," said James.

Aubrey's face lit up, "Are we going there?"

"Maybe," James pulled two suitcases off the baggage carousel.

"Mr. and Mrs. Nessumsar?" A man who appeared to be in his early twenties approached them. He extended his hand to James.

"Yes, that's us." James let go of the suitcase handle to shake his hand. He motioned to Alice and the kids, "Alice, Alex, and Aubrey."

"I'm Tony. Pleased to meet you," he shook Alice's hand as well. "Thanks for coming. I have a car right outside. It's only about an eight-mile drive to your hotel."

A man Tony did not introduce took the two suitcases. They followed Tony to the SUV parked at the curb and climbed in.

"We're going to Disneyworld," said Alex; he looked at his dad, "Maybe."

Tony laughed, "Sounds like a great plan to me."

"Thanks for having my back," James laughed.

Alice changed the subject, "Do we know what we're doing here?"

"*I* know," began Tony, "And you will tomorrow morning. We'll meet in your room tomorrow morning for breakfast when we'll have the debriefing."

"I won't be staying at the hotel with you folks, but I do have to ask you to stay in your room till morning. Just order room service for whatever you need."

"Mom said we're going to school?" Audrey wrinkled her nose.

Tony chuckled, "Just for a while. It will be fun."

Alex scoffed, "School isn't that fun."

"It's not that bad either," said Audrey.

Alex asked, "Can I play my games tonight?"

"Uh…" began James; he glanced at Tony. "We didn't bring them, son."

Alex looked mortified, "Why not?"

"How about I explain that in the morning? I promise I'll make it worth the time. Will that work?" asked Tony.

"Ugh, I guess so." Alex didn't look convinced.

James laughed, "You'll survive," he turned to Tony, "See you in the morning, and thank you."

Tony started for the door, then stopped. He reached into his backpack and handed James a cell phone. "This is a burner phone; your cells will be disabled in about an hour until you are on a plane for home."

Audrey whispered to her brother, "I hope we get to go to Disneyworld."

Alex whispered back," Me too."

Tony looked at the two kids and grinned, "Find what we're looking for, and Disneyworld is on me," he said quietly.

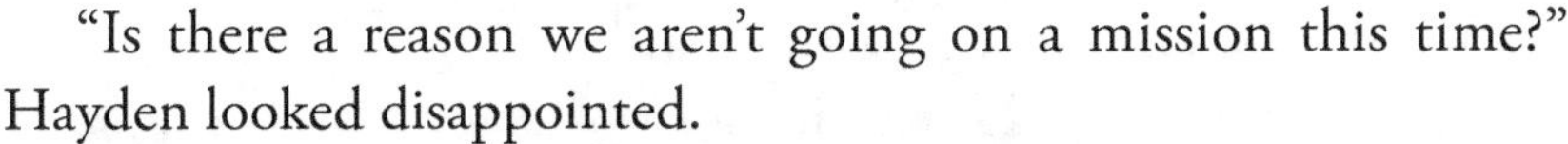

"Is there a reason we aren't going on a mission this time?" Hayden looked disappointed.

"Is it because she jumped out of the helicopter? Because I didn't. I *can* fly." Noelle seemed irritated.

"Geez, feeling a little guilty, are we? Lighten up, you two," Gunner frowned at them both. "Just because you're staying on the island doesn't mean you don't have an assignment."

Noelle rubbed her hands together, "Awesome, so what is it?"

Gunner chuckled, "Follow me."

When the three were seated in front of one of the computer screens in the bowery, Craig typed in some codes, and the screen lit up.

"Are we hunting bats?" Haydee scowled at the three different bat species.

"Nope," Craig reached past Haydee and typed some code on another keyboard, causing a second screen to light up—the same images appeared. "Researching. I need some thorough research on bats that might be—well, in Egypt, here, in the States. Which ones might be found in all three of those places—that's what I need to know."

Haydee and Noelle both looked puzzled, "Why? We only saw them in Egypt," said Noelle.

"A gut feeling."

"About?" asked Hayden.

Gunner sighed, "I'm not sure."

Haydee and Noelle exchanged a quick glance.

"I know, not much to go on. But start and keep track of everything you find. Maybe use an Excel spreadsheet—we need details."

"We?"

Gunner looked at Noelle, "I—I need them."

They both nodded.

"Okay, I'll check back in a few hours. Take breaks when you need to." Gunner started to walk away.

"Where are our parents?" asked Haydee.

"All of your parents, except James and Alice, took the yacht to pick up supplies. They'll be gone a day or two."

"Okay. Did Grandma go with them?"

Gunner added, "I don't think so. I believe she's on the other side of the island. But I'll be here; I'm working from Biorn's bungalow now."

"You know we've been on the island before alone," said Noelle.

"I'm not here to babysit, girls; I'm here to work. We'll collaborate on our info later."

"Got it." Noelle turned back to the computer.

Haydee glanced over her shoulder when Gunner walked away. She gasped, and Noelle looked up, "What?"

"I—I swear, Gunner lit up—or something."

"Excuse me?"

"He kind of faded to like iridescent, then back to normal."

Noelle turned to look in Gunner's direction, but he was now out of sight. She asked her cousin, "Do we need to be worried?"

"Probably not; maybe I need some sleep." she laughed but added, "After all, Noelle, we're not ones to be questioning abnormalities in others."

Noelle sighed, "Ya, I know."

The uneasiness wouldn't leave Haydee. She returned to her computer and punched some words into a Google search. Bat images started to appear. She glanced behind her again.

I wish Dad were here.

❧ 9 ☙

CONCERNS

BROOKE SIGHED, "Seems weird to have all the kids out on assignment simultaneously."

The butcher handed twenty-five pounds of cooked shrimp over the glass counter, and Aiko took it. She put it in the shopping cart, and the two moved toward the beef section.

"It will be hard for me to get used to the kids not having cell phones when on assignment. I'm used to checking in with my kids every day." Brooke began inspecting the steaks.

Aiko agreed, "It's especially Brighton; she's all over the place."

"She seems like she's grown up a lot, though."

She has for sure; Biorn says I worry too much," Aiko sighed.

Brooke smiled and put her arm around her sister-in-law's shoulder. "Well, I get it; my kids are older."

"The first year was, though odd, a little easier. Just random cases, and they were always with CIA or FBI agents; this will be different."

"How?" Brooke asked.

Aiko laughed, "More organized, maybe, more intense? I'm wondering about Gunner. He seems nice enough, and his credentials are impeccable, but…"

"But what?" Tatiana walked up to the two women.

"We were just talking about Gunner," said Aiko.

Tatiana waited for Aiko to continue.

"Just that it's kind of weird for him to be running things."

"Is that a bad thing?"

Brooke shook her head, "No, we just have to get used to it."

"I think it will be great." said Tatiana.

"What do you think of Gunner?" asked Brooke.

"He's, ummm, commanding," laughed Tatiana.

Aiko laughed, "He is that." She shrugged, "I'm sure it will be fine. Brooke and I were just saying it seems weird for the kids not to have cell phones. Not to be able to reach them."

"I agree with that, but we do have the manuscripts of their missions," said Tatiana.

"That's true. I had forgotten about that. I'll check that out when we get back to the island."

"What time were we meeting for lunch?" asked Brooke.

The three women paid for their purchases and walked to the waiting SUV.

Brooke opened the hatch, and they placed the meat in a cooler containing dry ice.

"Lunch at one, then we're heading to the yacht," said Tatiana.

"Sounds good," Brooke closed the hatch; she turned to Aiko, "What's next on our list?"

Everyone busily stowed the purchases and prepared for the nearly hundred-mile trip to Mayajaal.

Richard guided the yacht away from the dock, then slowly made his way out of the marina into the open ocean.

Everyone else gathered around a small table on the main deck just below the bridge.

Biorn grabbed a water bottle and looked at his siblings and spouses, "Are there some concerns about Gunner?"

Aiko scowled at her husband, "Seriously? You know I've had questions."

"I do know that. Anyone else?"

"Not concerns, just different; seems like we were more involved before," said Janae, "That's all."

"It's like letting go again; it's weird," agreed Amanda.

"It is, but it's all going to be good. It will make more sense after this first mission?" Biorn assured them.

"So, from this," Emmett scanned his phone, "It looks like all the kids are working on the same mission?"

Biron nodded, "That's what I understand."

"Looks like a theft ring ran out of a small apartment in San Jose," said Emmett.

"Mexico?" asked Janae.

"California, but not all of the kids are there."

Janae twisted her mouth, "Hmmm, well then, where are they?"

≈ 10 ≈

GEIST

Gunner finished setting up the closed video meeting with the Nessumsar Family agents. The kids' parents gathered in the bowery and sat before the screen. From California, Mack, Spencer, Ava, Micah, and their contact Char. From Iowa Lock, Kitana, Brighton, and their contact Ilene. From Connecticut, Katie, Nate, Zion, and their contact Gabe. From Florida Alex, Audrey, their parents, James and Alice, and their contact Tony.

The screen booted up, revealing four screens with all the agents.

Gunner began with a brief hello and welcomed the four contacts. "I just saw all of you a day ago, so let's get down to business."

The screen went blank, except for a tiny corner where the four hotel rooms were minimized.

A tiny dot in the middle of the screen slowly grew until the image of a woman appeared.

With short, cropped hair, she seemed to be tall and very thin. She had a starfish tattoo on the left side of her neck.

"That's the lady we were shown yesterday, right?" Mack's voice came through the speaker.

"Yes, that's Eleanor Anderson, better known to family and friends as Ellie—but better known to us—and her followers— Geist," said Gunner. "To explain to the rest of you, she is based out of San Jose; we know that. Our computer expert is Frank Meres; he showed Geist to the group yesterday. We know that Haydee played soccer with Ms. Anderson at San Jose, so Haydee was not assigned to this operation."

Gunner paused; he brought the starfish tattoo in closer, "Something about that tattoo bothers me; can anyone see a bat in there?"

Silence.

"No? Okay, moving on." Gunner began typing, and the screen filled with a different image. A woman's soothing voice said, '*Welcome to Praxis, a journey of learning and exploration.*'

Immediately scenes appeared but changed quickly—a countryside, a city block, a mountain, the ocean, a playground, a college campus, a skyscraper, an island, a volcano, an airplane, a yacht, ziplining. The scenes went on and on and changed rapidly.

The voice kept talking during the entire scene change, '*Where do you want to go? What would you like to do? To become? To, see? To experience? To be, to be, to be…*' the last two words echoed over and over as the scenes kept rapidly scanning.

Suddenly the scenes stopped, and the word PRAXIS filled the screen. Then the voice, '*Choose your level and let's begin.*'

Gunner paused the screen, "And this is where it starts. Players choose a level. Usually, the first one to begin with. The game takes them through different challenges and scenarios—there is no killing like in many other games. Instead, it is conquering. A lot of it is extreme sports, ziplining, kayaking, mountain climbing, etc. It starts simple, then with each level, it gets more challenging. But doable. Players rack up points along the way—and like in various other games, their names are displayed on the main screen as winners in whatever level they conquered. But the challenges get more complicated. I believe it's level ten," Gunner checked his notes, "Yes, level ten; this is where they start learning how to steal, and again, it's subtle at first. A candy bar, a dollar from a parent's purse or wallet, or an item from a friend's backpack or car. But then it escalates from there. Pretty soon, they are learning to hack into bank accounts and actual banks sometimes."

Gunner skipped through screens to demonstrate how the following levels worked. Then he said, "Up until about six months ago, it appears she has only recruited college-age kids."

"May I ask a question?" asked Lock.

"Sure," Gunner paused the screen.

"Why only college students? Why not older people?"

"We can only assume it's because students are always on their computers. But to your point, Lock, she started into high school kids over a year ago and middle school maybe six months ago, and her revenue increased exponentially. That's what pulled her up on the FBI radar. But now she has crossed over into elementary-age kids, which is why we have Alex and Audrey and their parents in Florida. There are two elementary schools in one general area where we have seen activity."

"May I interject something here, Gunner?" It was Frank, the computer expert from California.

"Absolutely. Do you need the screen?"

"Yes, please."

"It's all yours."

Frank changed the image on the screen to a young boy, maybe twelve, sitting at his computer in his room. The boy had on a headset, but they couldn't hear what he was listening to.

Frank pulled up a soundtrack, but then he split it into three different tracks. "Listen to this crap."

The first track was engaging, upbeat music; the second track was a series of beats, and the third was the words *Praxis to be me*, over and over and over.

"Now, each of those tracks may not seem significant by themselves, but when they are put together, they become a problem and a highly effective method of subliminal messaging. Listen." Frank played the first track—just music—for approximately one minute. Then he added the second track—the beats—and said, "They are almost unnoticeable. In fact, they would be if we hadn't split the tracks and played together. They seem to be part of the music. But then, put all three together."

He played them all just as the listeners would hear them, and it sounded like music. But then he magnified the sound of the third track, the message—it was spoken in the exact rhythm of the beats.

No one said a word.

Finally, Frank broke the silence, "Can you understand the seriousness? Kids are in their rooms, at home, not even playing Praxis, maybe doing homework, but they have this playlist from Praxis in different places throughout the game; that smooth voice reminds the players to listen to the soundtrack. It's frightening."

"And effective," added Gunner, "Thanks, Frank." He clicked the keyboard, and the screen was filled again with the four hotel rooms and Nessumsar Family agents.

"Now, let's get to why you're where you are."

∾ 11 ∾

RACON

SULO FOLDED HIS ARMS across his chest and leaned back in his chair. He surveyed the team he had assembled. Young and old, all intertwined with the same family rivalry extending back six centuries.

Torsten, his loyal friend of over one hundred years, climbed the steps to the podium and took the chair beside him.

"Formulating a plan, my friend?"

"Right now, I'm thinking. Do you realize it's been since the 1600s when this rivalry started? I must put an end to the Relhi grandchildren."

Torsten glanced at the team and then turned back to Sulo. "You have the right group here; you should be able to destroy them."

"Every time I read the journals of my ancestors the fire burns hotter in my soul. The battle continued even after the inception of superpowers. My family, the Greblos,' were limited to shapeshift-ers, but the Relhi family were endowed with every existing super-power. Each member of the Relhi family was given at least one power until it reached Rannug Relhi. The sixteen-year-old did not want any part of the superpowers, and against his father's plead-ings, he left for America."

"The Rivalry continued; I take it."

Sulo nodded, "It has only increased my passion to rid the world of the Relhi family. Now I believe I have the means to do that."

Alpo squirmed in his chair, and Erikki laughed at him.

"I told you to be patient; the time is here," said Erikki.

"I know, I know, seems like all we have done is train and train…"

"I don't think you understand what we're up against," the deep voice came from behind the two boys.

Even though he was just two years older than them physically, Anders towered above Erikki and Alpo. His soul was over one hundred years old, and he was selected to perpetuate the Greblos clan, which originated from the Zahl family of Nordland. Only a few of those remained in the army of Sulo. Most had drifted away and eventually died as they did not hold up their end of the bargain when they were selected many years earlier.

Being advanced to one of Sulo's captains at seventeen, he made it a point to intimidate the younger soldiers whenever he had the chance.

Not one to be pushed around even by Anders, Erikki stood, "And what would that be? That we don't understand?"

Anders stepped toward Erikki, "You think because you can become a bat that you can handle what they throw at us. Well, you can't," he stopped talking. His eyes became distant as he seemed to be remembering something.

Ever persistent, Erikki demanded, "What?"

Anders shook his head slightly and seemed to focus again. He looked directly into Erikki's eyes. "You won't see them coming…"

A commotion at the front of the room drew everyone's attention. It seemed by instinct that Anders and several others who held his same rank immediately moved to the front, taking positions directly in front of Sulo and Torsten.

Sulo stood, extended his hand, and moved it from right to left. The massive army silenced, waiting for Sulo to speak.

"As you well know, this battle we are about to face has been going on for centuries. But we face a different enemy this time and on unfamiliar ground. The battle has always been fought in Norwegian territories, but this time, we are going to America to face an enemy we may not totally understand." Sulo paused. Whatever he was about to say seemed to weigh heavily on his mind.

After several minutes, he continued, "Our decision today has not been reached without much thought and consideration." He motioned to Torsten, who turned at the same time, clicking a remote control. A screen dropped down behind Sulo, and the image of a bat manifested.

Torsten said, "Reserved only for the higher ranks of the army, you will now all be commissioned with the same lethal power," he pointed a laser beam at the bat's wings, holding it steady on two little ridges on the underside and at the end of each wing.

"These are controlled with your mind. Preserve the energy. The electronic signal is called racon. It radiates a lethal charge to any living thing it touches."

Undiscernible conversation erupted from the group of men and women but stopped when Sulo raised his hand.

Torsten continued, "However, there is a limit. You only have so much of this energy; once you have used it, you will be powerless as it drains your own natural energy from you, rendering you almost helpless."

Sulo said, "Which is why it has been preserved, up until now, for those of higher ranks. We don't want anyone left behind."

A voice from the middle of the group asked, "What if that does happen?"

Torsten acknowledged the girl, "Good question, Linnea. If you have lost the energy, you will need to find shelter until you can rejuvenate, which can take up to four hours. It will happen faster if you stay out of sunlight. However, you will not have the electrons in your wings; you will revert to your current growth stage."

Linnea nodded, and a few murmurings could be heard.

Torsten clicked the remote again, and another image appeared on the screen. Heimdall, the senior Viking of the Greblos clan.

"Heimdall will come by tonight, and you will all be endowed. When you wake up, the power will be in your bat wings," said Torsten. "You will feel a slight numbness in the tips of your fingers; this is to be expected, but the power is only available to you in bat form."

Sulo reminded all of them, "Remember that you have already lived. Some hundreds of years ago, some transformed very recently. It does not matter. You are in this group because you are more than human; you are immortal, so there is no fear of death. It is imperative to remember that you cannot be killed, but you can be incapacitated for a time."

"In other words, don't be idiots," added Torsten.

Sulo chuckled and nodded, "Yes, let's all come back alive; as alive as we can be."

✥ 12 ✥

OPERATION PURLOIN

"CALIFORNIA, you are looking for Mel, Bryan, and Steve; your starting point is a High School in San Jose. Geist is based in San Jose, but we have multiple locations where she could be, so we need to pin that down. Frank is working on skip tracing. Mack, you're a new teacher, Ava and Micah's students, and Spencer, Ava's big brother."

"Iowa, Vicki, Gracie, Tommy. This is a middle school; Lock student, Brighton student aid, and Kitana, Lock's big sister."

"Florida, two little kids in each school. Alice, you are an office aide. You and Alex are looking for twins, Sheena, and Sean. James, substitute teacher, you and Arian look for Beth, Cash, and Lily."

"Connecticut, Zion is the student, Katie is the substitute teacher, and Nate is the big brother of Zion. Subjects are Marla, Tracee, and Brett."

"Okay, the object is to get close to these students. They are all involved with Praxis; we have confirmed that. None of their parents even have a clue; at this point, it does not seem that they do. Ava, Micah, Lock, Brighton, Zion. Get close to any of these kids, join them, and get involved in Praxis. It's the only way we are going to nail this woman." Gunner scrolled his phone screen, then looked up, "Alice and James, we need Alex and Audrey to do the same thing. But for them, they become friends; that's where they

55

need to start. Hopefully, they can also become part of Praxis, but I don't want to push that too much."

"Don't underestimate Alex. The kid is a gaming pro," said James.

"Yep, I knew that. I just wasn't sure how you would feel about it."

"I'm okay with it, Gunner. Alice will be nearby; it's not like they are going to the kids' houses."

"They shouldn't have to." Speaking to the entire group, he added, "We have provided you with laptops. They are scrubbed, except for an email account for communication with the students and Praxis," said Gunner.

"Your contacts have everything you need; take time today to get familiar with the areas, and your drivers will pick you up within the hour. Tomorrow, Operation Purloin gets underway." Gunner stood, put both hands behind his neck, leaned back, and stretched, "Get enrolled in school, and let's bust this loser. Contacts, we will meet at nine pm central time tomorrow night."

He clicked some keys, and the screen went blank.

Haydee and Noelle had been nearby watching the meeting.

"So, we keep researching bats?" Haydee twisted her mouth into a scowl.

Gunner looked at her and Noelle, "Yep, I feel something coming this way, and I need to know what we're dealing with."

"Why are you so sure it's bats?" asked Noelle.

"I'm not; it's just a hunch."

Haydee sighed, "Well, for what it's worth, neither of us has found any species of bats that can get as big as the ones we saw in Egypt."

"But you did see them; they did attack you?"

Noelle nodded, "Yes, they were all different sizes, but the big ones were huge."

"Okay, then they do exist, right?"

Haydee and Noelle exchanged a quick glance, and then Noelle said, "Yes, I guess they do."

"Don't guess, Noelle, facts. Let's get the facts."

Haydee asked, "How long will they be gone?"

"Up to two months, maybe less. It depends on how long it takes." Gunner squinted and smiled, "But I have a surprise for you two."

"What?!" they said in unison.

"Later," and he walked away.

☙ 13 ❧

SCHOOL

To look inconspicuous, James and Alice needed cars to drive to the schools. There was only one car when the driver and Tony dropped them off.

James was puzzled, "I thought we were going to different schools?"

"I did, too," said Tony. "That changed about twenty minutes ago. Your assignments haven't changed but at the same school. There must be a reason; it came from Gunner."

Principal Glen Parker held his office door open for the new substitute teacher and office aide. "I wasn't aware you had children; did they get enrolled this morning?" He motioned to two chairs in front of his desk but remained standing.

"Yes," said James, "They are both headed to their classes. I can't believe how this came together. This is just a temporary job for Alice, well for me too, I guess, but it's great that we can be at the same school as our kids."

"I'm happy it worked out for all of us. Jenny, our office aide, is on maternity leave, so this is perfect timing for you, Mrs. Nessumsar."

"It's Alice, and yes, perfect timing."

Mr. Parker picked up two papers from his desk and handed them to James. "This month, it is Miss Crimson's class, sixth graders; she was in a car accident, and it may be a month before she can return to work. You also have a free period computer lab."

James laughed, "So free period...?"

"Yeah, you don't get one. It's called a free period, though." Mr. Parker seemed a little stressed, "None of us get one. School is nothing like when I started teaching fifteen years ago." He sighed, "We are short on staff like everyone else, so we all pull double duty around here. While you are in the computer lab, your students will be aiding the younger kids with a science lab in Mrs. Granger's class."

"I believe that's Audrey's teacher," said Alice, but then she clarified, "Audrey is our daughter."

Mr. Parker nodded briefly, and then James said, "And what do we do in the computer lab?"

"I have no idea; most kids know computers better than adults. Several different projects are going on in there."

"And who do I work with or report to?" asked Alice.

"Oh," Mr. Parker walked toward the open office door, and James and Alice followed.

"Mrs. Bentley!"

A short, plump woman, maybe in her mid-sixties, popped up behind a computer screen. "Yes, Mr. Parker."

"Oh, there you are, sorry to yell. This is Alice; she will be replacing Jenny for a while."

Mrs. Bentley scurried from behind the desk and rushed toward them. She grabbed Alice's hand in both of hers and grinned. Her cheeks seemed to glow, "Just call me Sadie; my real name is Sabrina. I'm not sure how it got shortened to Sadie, but it happened when I was a little girl."

Alice smiled, and the image of 'a right jolly old elf' came to her.

Sadie shooed Mr. Parker and James away with her hand, "Now you two get on—I've got this."

Mr. Parker laughed, "C'mon, James, I'll show you to your classroom; I can tell when I'm being dismissed." As they walked into the hallway, he said, "Sometimes I'm not sure who the principal is, me or Sadie."

James laughed, and Mr. Parker added, "Your classroom is room ten, right at the end of the hall. The bell's about to ring."

They entered the door, where at least thirty kids were milling around. James was pleasantly surprised to see Alex in his classroom. He asked Mr. Parker, "Is this a conflict? My son is in this class."

"No, you're not his permanent teacher. It's not uncommon to have students in the same class as a parent who is subbing. Let me know if you have any problems with it."

"We'll be okay."

Alex looked up, saw his dad, and grinned. With his eyes, he motioned to the boy next to him. James noticed but did not acknowledge it. The boy appeared shy and a bit awkward. It seemed that he and Alex had already made a connection.

The Overlook High School front desk lady had a kind face, "I have your paperwork here, Zion, and this is?" she motioned to Nate.

"This is my brother, Nate," said Zion.

Nate said, "Our mom started her new job today, so I'm here instead. I think she emailed Zion's paperwork."

"She did. I'm Mrs. Sanders; nice to meet you both," she handed Zion a slip of paper, "your schedule. The first period starts in ten minutes."

"Thanks." Zion took the schedule, and he and Nate left the office.

Nate looked around at the hallway filled with many diversified students, "Good luck," he said.

Nate gave Zion a quick salute. "See you after school, little bro."

Zion rolled his eyes. "Yeah." He walked over to an empty desk and sat down. He looked at the kid beside him, "Is this desk taken?"

"Nope, guess it's yours."

"Cool," Zion glanced up when the teacher walked into the room; he looked at the other kid again, "Zion."

"Lance. Looks like you play football."

"Yeah,"

"Cool, we could use another player."

Zion nodded, "cool."

"This way. Happy to have you aboard, Coach. Sorry, the swim coach position wasn't open just yet. He may need an assistant in a month or two, depending on if Coach Perry moves out of state after he gets married." They reached a classroom door, and Vice-Principal Jenkins opened it and waited for Mack to enter.

"It's okay; I'll hold out for the assistant, and in the meantime, I'm happy to have a job. Just got into town, so science it is."

"Great, we need you. We have a great bunch of kids here; top of district."

"Wow, hope I can keep up."

Vice-Principal Jenkins laughed, "I'm sure you'll be fine.

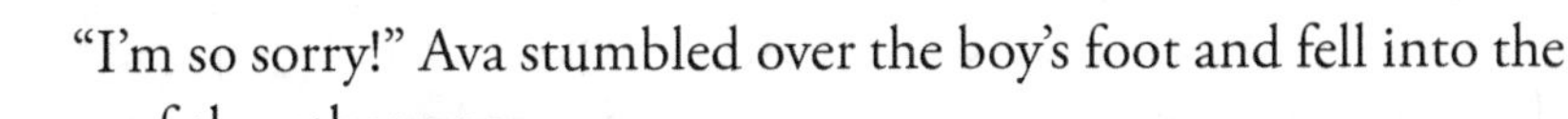

"Thanks for the lift!" Ava walked backward as she waved to Spencer.

He pulled his motorcycle away from the curb and slowly rolled out of the drop-off circle in front of the high school.

"Are they both there?" Char's voice came through the headset in Spencer's helmet.

Spencer glanced back before pulling onto the street just in time to see Ava crash into two guys. He laughed, "Well, Ava made an entrance."

He looked around, "Don't see Micah yet."

"Hang out there until you know she's there."

"Yep." Spencer pulled the bike to a stop against the curb. He watched intently through the helmet's rearview mirror.

"I'm so sorry!" Ava stumbled over the boy's foot and fell into the arms of the other one.

The boys both laughed, "No problem," the guy with the dark hair caught her arm.

"I'm Ava," she was still laughing."

"Rob," the same kid grinned, "You're new here, aren't you?"

"Yes, today."

"Nice entrance. I'm Bryan."

The three walked together toward the front doors.

"Where's your first period?" asked Rob.

"Not sure, room 115?"

"Ahh, Bryan can walk you; I'm in the computer lab today."

"Okay, well, nice to meet you," she walked with Bryan but stopped and whirled around, "Wait, the *day* in the computer lab?"

"Yep! All day!" Mel laughed and trotted down the hall.

"Have you seen Micah yet?" Char's voice came through the helmet mic again.

"No, I'll go find her."

"How?" Char demanded. "You can't go in there."

"Trust me."

"But…"

Spencer pulled his helmet off, disconnecting the headset. He climbed off the bike and walked toward a tree, scanning the school grounds for anyone who may see him.

The bell rang, but no one was around.

Spencer closed his eyes, clenched his fists, and faded until he was invisible. He ran to the front doors and looked at the security camera.

Here goes nothing.

Spencer pushed the door open, walked into the vestibule, and waited. A woman was coming toward him. He stood still; when she came out, he hurried in through the open door before it closed.

He walked down the halls completely unnoticed. He had Micah's schedule and knew her first class was math. He peeked in the open doors of several classrooms, but nothing.

He went down another hall; the first class on the left had algebra on the board.

I hate algebra.

There was Micah in the second row, third desk back.

He knew she couldn't see him but glared at her anyway. He started to walk away, then he stopped.

Oh, wait, this is too good.

He turned around and walked directly to her desk. She wore beanies, and one was sitting on her desk.

Spencer stopped; he picked the beanie up and dropped it on her desk.

Micah jumped, staring at the beanie. Then she squinted her eyes, looking around. She noticed the girl beside her looking at her from the corner of her eye. Micah smiled.

Spencer couldn't resist; he picked up the beanie and dropped it on the floor. It was all he could do not to laugh when Micah practically fell off her chair picking it up.

The girl beside her leaned back, obviously startled, and stared first at the beanie, then at Micah, who pulled the beanie practically over her eyes and slid down in her seat.

I'm going to kill Spencer.

Spencer climbed back on his bike and became visible again without checking his surroundings.

"What was that...?!"

Spencer whirled around.

Char stood in the middle of the road, her eyes wide, her mouth gaping open.

❦ 14 ❧

CONNECTIONS

"So, lab all day? How does that happen? What in the world do you do *all day* in there?" Ava popped a pickle in her mouth that had fallen from her hamburger onto her plate.

Mel eyed her, "Are you a computer nut?"

She smiled, "I'm trying to learn games to play them with my little brother. Can you help me with that?"

"Wait, what about me? I'm actually pretty good at gaming."

"Oh, this is my new friend Micah," she turned to Mel, "This is Mel." She looked across the table, "And Bryan."

"Hey, Micah," Bryan grinned at her.

Mel nodded at Micah, "So you're good at gaming?"

"Pretty good. I have things to learn, but, yeah, I'm good."

Mel and Bryan locked eyes but said nothing.

Micah broke the silence, "So, do you teach computers, gaming, what?"

"And to whom?" asked Ava.

"I don't teach as much as assist the teacher. I'm pretty good…"

"Computers are his life." Said Bryan.

"Not my life, I'm just good at them, that's all."

The bell rang, and they all stood, threw their wrappers in the trash, and started toward the hall.

A girl approached them and looked right at Mel, "Going to introduce me?"

"Oh, yeah. Britt, this is Micah and Ava - Ava just started here," he turned to Micah, "Are you new too?"

"Yes, Ava and I are the newbies in the first period."

"Where did you move from?" Britt demanded.

"What difference does it make?" Mel seemed annoyed.

"It's okay, I'm from Utah," said Micah.

"California," said Ava.

Britt glared at each of them, turned and walked away.

❧ 15 ❧

CLOSE ENCOUNTERS

Ava couldn't get out of class to go to the computer lab; neither could Micah, so they arranged to meet with Mel right after school.

When they went in, Mel was sitting on a stool next to a man who appeared to be a teacher.

"Hey, there you are glad you could make it," he introduced the man as Mr. Cutler, the Keeper of the lab.

They laughed, "Not a teacher?"

"Of course," said Mr. Cutler, "But I prefer the Keeper of the lab. Sounds cooler."

Mel stood, "I have two computers over here for you guys."

"Are they ready for a game?" asked Micah.

"Yep, sign in and choose a username."

Micah laughed, "I'm choosing Kitty." She signed into the game and put in her name.

Micah chuckled at Ava's reference to her morphing superpower. She typed her pretend name. Imagine that.

Micah leaned over and looked at Ava's screen, "Imagine that?"

"Yeah," she laughed.

The screens lit up, and the players were listed in the center of the screen.

The first was 'Kitty,' the second was 'Imagine That', and the third was 'Keeper.'

"So, you're Keeper?" asked Ava.

"Nope, I'm Vulture."

"Then who's Keeper?" asked Ava.

"A friend. He doesn't like anyone to know who he is."

"Hmm, I didn't think some games allowed anonymity."

"Some do, some don't. But it's cool, I know him."

Micah glanced at Ava out of the corner of her eye. Ava read that as *drop it*—so she did.

Ava wiggled her fingers above the keyboard, "So now what?"

Micah pointed to the screen, "As soon as all the players are listed, Mel will start the countdown—once it does, you're in the game, and you start playing."

Mel said, "These are all gaming consoles, some of the latest equipment PS4. Those two over there," he pointed to two consoles on the table behind them, "Those are Xbox."

"I can't believe you have gaming consoles in school," said Micah, "How come this school has them?"

Mel shrugged, "Mr. Cutler's idea."

Mr. Cutler walked up behind them, "My thinking was, and to clarify, it was no easy task to get past the school district; if the kids want to learn computers, and they like gaming, this is a great way to get them interested."

He put his hand on Mel's shoulder, "It's worked. Right, Mel?"

"Yep, it's been great! Okay, Keeper is ready to start the game."

"What am I supposed to do?" asked Ava.

Mr. Cutler moved closer to Ava and pointed to her screen, "That's you; you're trying to get that guy with the weird ears." He handed her the controller, "Those buttons move left, right, etc. You know that, right?"

Ava nodded, "Of course. I know that much," she laughed.

"Okay," said Mr. Cutler, "This is your strike button. When you are ready to take a shot, click that."

"You have to be fast," said Micah. "Don't take your eyes off the screen."

Ava tried keeping up with the other three players, but suddenly, her character fell into a heap of little pieces.

"What the heck?" Ava's eyes widened. "What happened? My person won't move."

"You're dead," laughed Micah.

"Who killed me?"

A voice came through the speaker, "That would be me." The voice was low and sounded like a robot?

"Who are you?" Ava leaned into the screen.

The same computer robot-like voice again said, "Keeper."

"Dang! I hardly got to play!"

"I'm not going to be here much longer either," said Micah, "These guys are ruthless!"

"You're hanging in there, though." Almost as soon as Mel spoke, Micah's character dissipated.

"Ahhh! I'm dead."

"There's always next time," said Keeper.

"Is he laughing? He's laughing!"

Mel chuckled, "Probably, he does that."

"I thought you could play these games for hours. That was short," said Ava.

"Well, you can play for hours if you're good," said Micah.

"How do you practice? Can you practice without playing in a game?" asked Ava.

"It's better just to play the game repeatedly," said Mr. Cutler.

"You can learn skills by playing many different games, too," added Mel.

Mr. Cutler looked at Mel, and they locked eyes for a few seconds, and then Mr. Cutler nodded.

Mel said, "We have a new game you might want to learn. It might be easier for you, Ava, since it's a startup; there's not much competition."

Ava shrugged, "What do you think?"

"Why not?"

There was a brief knock on the open door, "Mr. Cutler, right?"

They all turned toward the door, and Mack walked in.

"May I help you?" asked Mr. Cutler.

"I hope so," Mack nodded in the three kids' directions, "Hi." Then he continued, "I'm Mack Tanner. I'm a new teacher. I need to improve my computer skills, and Mr. Jenkins suggested I talk to you."

Mr. Cutler stood, "Sure, I'm happy to oblige, and welcome to Jenkins High."

"Thanks." Mack didn't look at either of his cousins again.

"When would you like to get started?" asked Mr. Cutler.

"I just moved here, so I'm free any day after school except for Thursdays."

"Ahh, yes, faculty meeting."

"Yeah, but any other day."

Mr. Cutler pulled out his phone and scanned through the screen for a few seconds. Then he asked Mel, "When do we meet next?"

"Tomorrow night at six."

With Steve? Micah wondered.

"Okay, Mack, today is Tuesday. I have time right after school tomorrow but must be done by five thirty."

"Sounds good to me. Should I meet you here?"

"Yes, around three-thirty or so. I may have students here till then."

"Good deal, thanks, Mr. Cutler."

"You can call me Jon."

"Thanks, Jon, see you then," said Mack, and he left.

Mel said, "I have to head out. See you two tomorrow at school?"

Both girls nodded, and Ava glanced up at the wall clock, "It's five-thirty. Wow, we've been here for two hours. That went fast."

"Time flies…"

Ava squinted at Mel, "Please don't say when you're having fun. I didn't do much that was fun."

Mel laughed, "You will," and his eyes twinkled.

Ava and Micah left the school to wait for Spencer to pick Ava up.

"Hey," it was Bryan, "Sorry I missed the gaming lesson. I had study hall."

"After school?" asked Micah.

"Yeah, I don't have a free period since I spend it in the computer lab."

"The computer lab gets lots of attention, doesn't it?"

Bryan said, "Yeah, lots of reasons. It can be lucrative."

"How's that?" asked Ava.

"Some of us play games for money, not a lot of money, but you don't need a lot in high school, so it seems like a lot." Bryan chuckled, "I just said a lot, a lot."

They all burst out laughing.

"I wasn't going to point that out." Micah was still laughing.

Bryan changed the subject, "Are you guys waiting for a ride?"

"I am," said Ava. "Hey Micah, why don't you text your mom? My brother can take you home since she's not finished at the dentist."

"Okay," Micah pulled out her phone.

"I was going to say I can take you both home."

"Thanks, Bryan, but my brother would kill me, and so would my dad."

"You got that right." The voice came from behind them where Spencer had just materialized.

"Holy cow! Where did you come from?"

Enjoying that he had alarmed Bryan, Spencer said, "I was right there." He pointed to the flagpole, "I parked in a different place this time."

Ava glared at him, "All you had to do was text me."

"I know, but this is more fun."

"You didn't ride your bike, did you? I was hoping you could give Micah a ride."

Spencer turned toward the parking lot where his motorcycle was parked, "Uh…"

Instantly, a Range Rover sat where the motorcycle had been.

"Like I said, yeah, I brought the Range Rover."

Ava smiled smugly when Spencer looked at her.

"Bryan, this is my brother, Spencer."

"Sorry to startle you, man."

Bryan was not aware of the change in vehicles Ava had made. "No problem, nice to meet you." He told Ava and Micah, "I'll see you tomorrow."

Bryan turned to walk away and bumped right into Britt.

"Geez, what is it with people today?"

Britt looked at him quizzically, "I'm not sure what that means. Did you forget I'm riding with you to Steve's tonight?"

Bryan's face flushed, "Yeah, I guess I did. We'd better go, it's five till."

"Exactly." Britt turned on her heel, and, saying nothing more, Bryan followed her.

"She seems like a little spitfire," said Spencer.

Ava was still watching Britt and Bryan, "I actually have a couple of other words to describe her." She turned to Spencer, "That wasn't funny."

"What? Yes, it was!"

"It was kind of funny, Ava. Good that you're so fast making things appear and disappear. How would we have explained that one?"

The three were the only ones still on the school's front lawn, and they started for the parking lot.

Without warning, four men came from behind the Range Rover.

They walked directly toward the three; within a few feet of them, they morphed into small bats and flew at their faces.

Spencer immediately disappeared, coming up behind the bats; Ava stood firm but caused bright lights to surround her; Micah forced everything she could to morph into not a cat but a cougar. It lasted only seconds, though, and she fell faint on the grass.

The bright lights caused the bats to retreat as Spencer helped Micah to her feet.

"More practice," she said weakly, "I need more practice."

The three climbed in the Range Rover, and Spencer locked the doors. "Are you two, okay?"

"Yes," they said in unison.

"What made you think of the lights?" asked Spencer.

"It wasn't my first thought. I was trying to make an ultrasonic sound. I know they hate that, but it didn't happen, so I changed to lights."

"How did you know to do that?" asked Micah.

"After we met with Gunner the other day, I Googled bats and what they're afraid of. I didn't think I would ever have to use that information."

Spencer put both hands on the wheel, "I'm glad you did. What do you think they mean... the bats?"

Neither girl responded initially, but Micah said, "That's twice that we know of. Mack, Noelle, and Haydee, and now us."

"Something's up," said Ava.

Spencer started the engine, backed out, and pulled onto the street. In the rearview mirror, he saw the four bats behind them but didn't mention it. Seconds later, they were gone.

∽ 16 ∾

FAILED MISSION

"THAT WAS A FAILED ATTEMPT. I don't want to report this." Aric, a member of the Greblos Family army and the same age as Alpo was frustrated and wasted no words expressing his feelings to the other three.

Alpo agreed, "We must figure this out. Do you think Sulo or Torsten knows about these non-human powers these people have?"

The four team members sat in a restaurant in San Jose, California. Hedrick, and Ivar, sat aloof, saying nothing.

"I was surprised at their immediate response to us," said Aric.

"So was I. This is more of a challenge than I suspected. How about you, Alpo?"

"Agreed."

Alpo said, "I'm contacting Sulo now. Let's go back to the hotel and sleep until we get further orders."

❧ 17 ❧

OLIVER

"YOU ARE HUGE!" Lance slapped Zion on the back, "I'm glad you're on the field."

"You must be what? Six two, six three?" asked Brett.

"Six-two." Zion removed his helmet and rubbed his hand through his sweaty hair.

"Hey, big guy?"

"She's talking to you, dude." Lance pointed past Zion to the two girls walking towards them.

"Who?"

"Tracee, she and Marla are cheerleaders," said Lance.

Zion grinned when the girls walked up next to him. "I'm Tracee, and this is Marla. We're having a party Friday night after the game, interested?"

Zion glanced at Lance and then Brett, "Are you two going?"

"Sure, you should come; it's always a good time," said Brett.

"Okay."

"Want us to pick you up?" asked Brett.

"I just got a new car; I'd like to drive. Should we meet here and then go together?"

Lance and Brett exchanged a quick glance, then Lance said, "That works."

"Then it's a date," Tracee grinned, and the two girls walked away.

"Hardly a date," mumbled Zion.

"Group, group date."

Zion looked at Brett, "Gotcha."

The game was a solid win against Chaparral High, fourteen to six.

Two hours later, Zion pulled into the parking lot at the school. Lance and Brett were standing next to Brett's car.

They both climbed in, and Lance gave directions to Tracee's house. A dozen cars were already there.

The three walked into the crowded living room, where music blasted from the speakers, and kids were laughing and eating chips and salsa from a table in the kitchen. The smell of BBQ hamburgers permeated the air.

Tracee ensured Zion was introduced to everyone, but then they ate in the backyard. It was then that Oliver Hemming appeared.

He walked directly up to Zion, "Good to have you with our team, Zion, isn't it?"

Zion said, "Yes, but I haven't seen you at any of the practices."

Oliver looked around, "Oh, I don't play football. Tracee thought you might be interested in another team."

Zion's face was blank, "Not sure what you're talking about." He felt compelled to look towards some trees and was surprised to see Katie, but she disappeared again. Nate, too, and then he was gone. He was comforted to know they were there, but trying to figure out why was disconcerting.

What's going on?

Oliver motioned for Zion, Lance, Brett, and Tracee to follow him into the garage.

Tracee walked ahead and opened a door at the back of the garage.

Zion was surprised to see a room with four gaming consoles. When they were all inside, Tracee closed the door.

"Isn't this cool? My dad built this room for me for gaming. I can have three friends here, all simultaneously, for us to play. It's cool."

Zion had to agree; it was a cool room.

"It's not really something I get into, but Brett does," said Lance.

"I haven't played much either." Zion picked up a controller, "Let's go."

Oliver glanced over at Tracee and then Oliver said, "This is a new game. None of us have played it much."

Zion didn't have much experience in gaming at all, but Nate did. The screens lit up immediately, and gratefully for Zion, Nate squeezed into the chair with him. The room was dark, so no one noticed that Zions' hands were on the controller, but Nate was running it.

The game went fast. When it ended, Zion had come in second only to Oliver.

"Maybe we're ready for the next level," said Oliver.

Tracee turned to Brett, who agreed, "Yeah."

"You game, Zion?"

Zion couldn't see Nate, but he felt the squeeze on his arm, "Sure, let's try it."

"I think you've been holding out on us, Mr. Football," Oliver didn't look at Zion; he continued to look straight ahead.

Zion bristled, "Don't call me that. You don't even play football."

"Okay, okay, didn't mean to push your buttons."

"Well, you did. Are we going to play or not?" asked Zion.

Tracee said, "Hey, let's go back to the party. We can continue this another day."

"Okay, by me," Zion stood, pushing his chair back, almost knocking Nate on the floor.

He got a glimpse of Katie; she was smiling, but he didn't miss the obvious concern in her eyes.

Zion found Lance and sat down to eat a hamburger. He glanced over at Brett, who looked away.

Katie and Nate stood out in front of Tracee's house.

"What do you think?" asked Katie.

"I think we hit a nerve."

"You hit a nerve; we did nothing."

Nate sighed, "Well, I think we're closer. I can't wait until we regroup with the whole team. It would be nice to see where we're all at in this."

"Right? I hate that we can't communicate with each other."

"Mr. Nessumsar?"

"Who's asking?"

"I am," the man who walked out of the darkness slugged Nate in the gut, doubling him over."

Nate groaned and grabbed his stomach, but instinctively, he vanished, reappearing this time as a Viking in full armor.

His six-foot-five frame reared up, sword in hand.

The man started to run, and so did his partner, who had pushed Katie into the bushes. She scrambled to her feet just in time to see Zion run past her at lightning speed.

Zion caught the man in seconds, tackling him to the ground. "What's up with you, man? Who are you?"

Zion pulled the man to his feet, and Nate had the man who slugged him in a throat hold. The two intruders locked eyes, then suddenly, loud screeching and two bats streaked into the sky.

Both Nate and Zion stumbled.

"What was that?"

Katie ran up to them, "They were bats!"

"Holy…!" Nate pulled out his burner phone and called Frank.

"What's up?" Frank answered immediately.

"Bats, we got bats—we'll be there in fifteen minutes."

⤞ 18 ⤝

An Un-Birthday

ALICE PULLED UP to a mansion. She checked the address a second time. "Do I have the right address?"

Tony's voice came through the tiny speaker in Alice's ear. "Does it look like a small White House?"

"It's a sister White House."

Tony laughed, "That's it."

Alice pulled into the circular driveway and stopped. A young man in a suit walked up to her door and opened it, "Evening, ma'am."

"Hi," Alice stepped out of the car, "C'mon kids."

The same young man opened Audrey's door, and another opened Alex's. They climbed out, Audrey carrying a pink and yellow gift bag.

"Alex, where is Sean's gift?"

Alex moaned, "I don't want to carry it."

"Oh, good grief, give it to me."

Alice gave Alex a stern look; he stopped and climbed back into the car.

The young man looked at Alice and laughed.

Alex climbed back out and handed the gift to his mom.

Alice laughed, "I got you."

"Mom, I don't really like Sheena; she's kind of mean."

"Well, maybe she has a reason."

"There's no reason to be mean, Mom. That's what you always tell us," said Audrey.

"That's true, but we don't know anything about these kids, do we?"

"I guess, but Sean is a jerk, Mom; he doesn't even try to be nice," said Alex.

Curiously, Alice glanced around. There were no other cars parked out front.

She rang the doorbell and waited.

The door opened; a young woman stood in the doorway. "Come in, you can put the gifts over there, then follow me."

They walked through the massive entry, turned down a hallway, and then turned into another hallway that led through the kitchen.

It was then that Alice heard children's voices. They stepped into the backyard where easily fifty boys and girls played games, ate food, or jumped in the enormous blowup slide house.

A girl around nineteen approached them, "Hi, I'm Natalie, the kid's nanny. Please join in the fun. The birthday kids are not here yet."

"Sheena and Sean aren't here?"

"No, they haven't made it back yet. They had an appointment."

"An appointment?"

"I know, weird, right, but that's how this family is."

"Mom, can we go to the jump house?" asked Aubrey.

"Yes, go ahead." She asked Natalie, "Do they have other children?"

"No, just the twins. Well, their dad, Mr. Branson, has an older son. They were married kind of late. He's older, fifty-five, I think. She's maybe fifty-one or two."

Alice couldn't help but survey the yard. A spacious patio and firepit, a swimming pool no, two swimming pools, and trees and bushes. A beautiful yard that could pass for a park.

Suddenly feeling anxious, she checked to make sure she could see Alex and Audrey.

Natalie stood nearby, looking a little anxious.

Alice asked, "Will the kids be here or not? My kids just met them two weeks ago."

"I hope so; I don't want to entertain fifty kids by myself."

"Do you have other games? I can help you if you like."

"Minatare golf, there's a pickle ball court, they can go swimming if they want—we have lifeguards."

"Where are the other parents?"

"I don't know. Parents just drop the kids off. It's like this weird dynamic. My parents think I should quit. It's hard, though; my annual pay is a hundred thousand dollars."

Alice gulped, "What?"

"I know, right? I don't do much but take them shopping, to and from school; sometimes Joanne takes them if she's around."

"What about their dad?"

"Umm, he's in and out. I have a room here, an entire wing; it's an apartment."

"Nice."

"Yeah."

The kids played games, swam, and ate for the next two hours. Sheena and Sean still hadn't arrived.

"Well, I think we're going to take off. We are meeting my husband for dinner," said Alice.

Natalie sighed, "Okay, I'm sorry. The other kids will leave soon anyway; the party ends at five."

"How sad, they didn't even attend their own party."

"It doesn't matter, honestly. None of these kids even like Sheena or Sean."

Alice frowned, "What? I guess I don't understand."

Natalie said, "It's complicated. These kids don't need anything; the party is for show. I'm not sure why, but the kids don't care."

Alice looked sideways at Natalie, "Maybe they do."

Natalie said, "What do you mean?"

"Maybe they do, but they aren't given a chance." Alice shrugged, "I'm sorry, it's none of my business. I shouldn't pry."

"No, I get it."

Alice called, "Audrey, Alex, let's go!"

They both came from the miniature golf course, and Audrey said, "Hey, they didn't come to their party."

"I told you they're weird." Alex grabbed a soda from the cooler. He looked at Natalie, "It's okay, right?"

"Of course, that's what they're for. Do you guys want to take some cake and ice cream?"

Both Alex and Audrey declined.

"We're going to eat with our dad," said Alex.

Alex started to walk through the kitchen but stopped, "How do we get out of here?"

"I'll show you," said Natalie.

The young man brought the car around, and Alice handed him a ten-dollar bill.

"It's okay, ma'am."

"I insist."

"Okay, thank you."

When Alice pulled the car out of the circular driveway, Tony came through the speaker, "How did it go?"

"A birthday party with no birthday kids. A little strange."

Suddenly, Alice screamed and slammed on the brakes.

"Alice, what is it? Alice!"

"What was that Mom?" screamed Audrey.

"They looked like bats, a million bats!" Alex was leaning over the front seat.

Alice stared out the windshield. The air was clear, only a black cloud in the distance. She hadn't moved the car.

"Alice?"

"We're okay, Tony, sorry. As soon as my heart gets back in my chest."

"Okay, let's not talk about it now. Can you get to the hotel?"

"Yes, but we're supposed to meet James for dinner."

"I'm here." James's voice came through the speaker.

"James!" Alice called.

"Yes, I'm here. I, uh, are you guys, okay?"

"We are," said Alice. "You sound odd though—are you okay?"

James hesitated, "I had *my own* bat encounter."

19

REGROUP

ALPO PULLED UP the screen, "Sulo?"

"We have decided to regroup. We want you all back here tomorrow."

Alpo lowered his head, "I'm sorry, Sulo."

"Do not be sorry. Each team had problems. We will meet and figure out our next move."

"Just come home." Torsten's voice came through the speaker, and his face appeared on the screen.

"Okay."

"Your tickets will be waiting for you at the airport."

"Yes, Sir." Alpo turned off the monitor, and the screen went black.

"Back to Norway." Alpo sighed and looked at his team, "Going home for now."

20

SECRETS

Tommy caught up with Brighton, "Hey, what have you got going on after school today?"

"I'm…I don't know, what do you have in mind?"

"I have a friend who has started this cool gaming party. We meet on Thursdays right after school."

"Does this friend have a name?" asked Brighton.

"Yeah, Gracie Turnbow. We've been playing for a couple of months. Just give it a try."

"I'm not sure I want to hang out with a bunch of middle school kids."

"There is a method to my madness."

Brighton eyed him, "What would that be?"

"I have a brother, Clay; I told him about you. He'll be there too."

"What makes you think I want to meet your brother?"

Tommy shrugged, "I just thought it would be fun."

"Okay, fine, I'll come. Sounds fun."

"Great, I'll get her address to you. It's close, only a few blocks away."

Brighton smiled, "Thanks for the invite. Now get to class," she snickered, "I love being a teacher's aide."

"Well, for the sake of students everywhere, please don't become a teacher. Maybe a real estate agent or an attorney."

"Oh, please," she walked away, "Get to class."

"Okay, bye! Have a great day, happy person!"

Brighton waved and disappeared around the corner.

Tommy walked into his fourth-period class, sat beside Gracie, and pulled the microscope closer to his space. "What do we have here?"

"I'm not sure; I need to get the specs," said Gracie.

"Hey, I got that new teacher's aide to come Thursday. Her name is Brighton."

"How did you do that?"

"Told her my brother would be there."

"Wow, okay."

"How many do we need—I mean, how many did he tell you?"

"Six, we have five."

"Did you ask Vicki? You know she wants to participate in anything you do."

Gracie scoffed, "I don't know…"

"C'mon, just because she's your cousin?" Tommy chuckled.

"She's not very good at secrets."

"What secrets?" Lock walked over to their table.

"How long have you been standing there?"

"Long enough," Lock laughed. "So, is this a secret party?"

"Kind of," Gracie pulled a face. "We don't even know why."

"What kind of party is it?"

"It's gaming—Gracie said you like gaming."

"I do. I'm good at it, not pro, but good."

"Then you'll fit right in," said Tommy.

"Who's the guy demanding you have six, and why six?" asked Tommy.

"I'm not sure. We're going to be working with some other kids," said Gracie. "According to a friend of mine it can be good money."

"What friend?" asked Lock.

"His name is Oliver. I barely know him."

"But money?" asked Lock.

"Apparently. Guess we'll find out."

Lock shrugged, "Cool."

He went back to his table, pulled out his phone and typed a note—*Oliver and Vicki*. He already knew who Brighton was.

❧ 21 ☙

REPORTS

"CAN YOU BRING that screen up, Haydee?"

Gunner sat in front of the big console with Haydee and Noelle on either side.

"Sure," Haydee pressed some buttons, and the colossal screen lit up.

"You both have pictures of what you found, right?"

Noelle said, "So far, we've found fifty different species, but there are over fourteen hundred in the world, and yes, we have pictures for most of them."

"They can be as large as a small dog or as small as a bee," said Haydee, "One has a wingspan of five feet!"

Gunner looked surprised, "Really? I had no idea."

"I was shocked—and it's freaky," said Noelle.

"I can't argue with that—what I'm trying to figure out is why are they attacking you kids?"

Gunner clicked a button, and all four teams appeared on the screen. "So, what's going on?"

"I'll go first if that's okay," said Craig.

Gunner said, "I know there have been some encounters with bats, whatever is going on, but I'd like reports first on our mission. What do you have?"

Craig glanced at Zion, who seemed disappointed that the meeting was going in that direction.

"So far, our team has made a connection with a kid named Lance; he's actually quarterback on the football team and took an immediate interest in Zion for obvious reasons," Craig chuckled, "Zion is on the team now and playing first-team defense. They are going to be disappointed when he leaves."

"Marla and Tracee—Tracee is the key person here, not Marla. Tracee has a gaming room in her dad's garage. She also introduced Zion to Oliver; he was an unexpected contact and seemed to play a key role. We are not sure how key, but he seems to be important. Brett is Lance's friend, also on the football team, and into the gaming scene, but it's hard to tell if he is involved beyond simply being a gamer."

Craig glanced at his team, who seemed to agree, "All that being said, we're focusing on Tracee and mostly Oliver."

Gunner nodded, "Good work; follow up?"

"I'm sure I'll be invited to a gaming party again soon; if not, I'll ask, but Oliver seems intense, so our plan is for me to go indirectly through Tracee to him."

"Bats?"

Nate said, "These were two men who ambushed Katie and me in the front yard of Tracee's house, where the party was being held. I'm stressing men because they turned into bats when we retaliated."

"Turned into…?"

The screen became a buzz of conversation, "Whoa, one at a time." Said Gunner, "Go on, Nate."

But it was Katie who spoke up, "Two men attacked Nate and me. We both vanished, but then we fought back, and the minute we did, they began screeching an unearthly sound, morphed into bats, and were gone instantly."

Gunner waited for Nate or Zion, but all Nate said was, "What she said."

"Uh, how big were the men? I mean, before they became bats?" asked Haydee.

Gunner interjected, "Haydee and Noelle are researching bats for me; there are more species than I ever imagined."

Nate, Katie, and Zion were talking when Craig said, "Apparently they were small—the bats—once they were no longer—human?"

Gunner laughed, "Having a hard time with this, are we?"

Craig raised his eyebrows, "You mean that I am living in a world that I had no clue existed?"

Gunner chuckled but said, "Okay, Ilene, what's happening in Iowa?"

"Well, there is corn growing," mumbled Lock.

Kitana smacked him on the arm, "Will you get over the corn thing?"

Gunner waited…

Ilene said, "Lock met Gracie, Katie met Tommy; we learned that Gracie and Tommy are friends. Gracie invited them to a gaming party that hadn't happened yet. But Tommy invited his brother, Clay, who is Brighton's age. They keep mentioning a 'him' who wants six new game players. Brighton met the Vice Principal, whose name is Ember Hunter, and prefers the kids call her Ember." She looked at her team, "Am I forgetting anything or anyone?

Kitana said, "Vicki is not really a person of interest at this point. We're unsure how she fits in, but she is Gracie's cousin and apparently can't keep a secret." Also, Gracie has a friend, Oliver. She mentioned him."

Lock chimed in, "No bats here. Only corn."

They all laughed, but Brighton said, "This is such a laid-back community. Everyone is kind of private, so getting close is hard."

"I think Tommy hopes you and Clay will be close," Lock chided.

"Well, we don't know that do we? We haven't met Clay," added Brighton, "Gracie talks about that Oliver guy Kitana mentioned. It seems like he might be older than her."

Ilene said, "One thing that may be pertinent to this is that apparently, these kids earn money when they play the game."

"They get paid?" asked Gunner.

"No, we can win the game; I'm not sure how it works yet," said Lock.

"I think that's it, Gunner," said Ilene. "Oh, and Lock told the kids his real name is Lawrence, in case that comes up; that's about it. kind of…"

"Borrrr—innngggg." Lock slumped in a chair.

Gunner nodded, "Hang in there. At least you have the potential to make money when you play. Char, what you got for us?"

Char brought her usual demeanor to the call, completely un-emotional.

"Mel and Bryan are good friends and have become friends with Ava and Micah. Mack is subbing in a class for a couple of months; he connected with Mr. Cutler, who runs the computer lab and prefers to be called Keeper of the Lab," She looked directly into the camera at Gunner, "Just weird."

Mack added, "I made it a point to ask Mr. Cutler for help on my computer, seeing him this week. We are not exactly sure what Mr. Cutler…"

"Keeper of the Lab," said Ava.

"Yeah, but he told me to call him Jon." Mack continued, "We aren't sure if there is any connection, but KOTL—that's easier to say, might be intertwined somehow. Mel spends a lot of time with him in the computer lab, and so do a lot of other kids."

Char said, "Britt definitely has some involvement, according to Micah and Ava."

Micah said, "She sure seems to. She's demanding and sarcastic, pretty much tells Mel and Bryan where it's at, and then there's Steve."

"Steve?" Gunner seemed to listen more intently.

"Yes," said Char, "He appears to be the mastermind of the entire gaming thing, at least at this school."

"He's a scrawny, short kid, seems more like a nerd than any kind of tough guy, but Mel and Bryan listen to him," said Ava.

"We played one game, and there was this player, Keeper," said Micah.

"The same Keeper as in the lab guy?" asked Gunner.

The girls looked at each other, and Ava said, "It couldn't be Mr. Cutler. He was with us during the game and not playing anything, just watching."

"But that's an interesting coincidence," said Mack.

Gunner leaned forward, "So, Char, tell me about—superpowers."

Char's face turned bright red. "Well, I believed it was all nonsense, but I saw Spencer materialize right before my eyes. I'm still trying to comprehend it. That's all I've seen, but it seems they are real—at least his."

Mack scoffed, but no one acknowledged.

"Spencer, who freaked out your handler? Tell me about bats." Gunner looked over at Noelle and Haydee. "Pull some of those pictures up on your screens and be ready to project them here."

"Okay," said Haydee, and Noelle nodded.

"We, me, Ava, and Micah, were in front of the school; no one else was around. This, by the way, after Ave turned my motorcycle into a Range Rover…"

Spencer caught Gunner's questioning look and added, "That's another story. Anyway…"

"And after you freaked Bryan out," said Micah.

"Yeah, well, the three of us were walking toward the parking lot, and three guys showed up out of nowhere. They walked in our direction, but just before they reached us, they all turned into bats and flew right at our faces. I disappeared and…"

Micah interrupted, "I failed to morph into a cougar but fell on the ground instead. It was Ava who got them off us."

"How?" asked Gunner.

"I tried a high-frequency sound but couldn't make it happen fast enough, so I did bright lights. When we were in Mayajaal I Googled what bothers bats in case we ever needed to know. I think we might need it even more than I thought we would," said Ava.

"Good thinking, Ava; and the bats?"

Spencer looked at his cousins and then back at Gunner. "They flew away. Fast.'

Gunner slowly nodded; he motioned to Noelle, and images of bats appeared on the screen so everyone could see them.

"Did the bats that any of you saw look like these?"

The images scrolled slowly on the screen while Char and Craig's teams shook their heads.

James started to say something, but Gunner held his hand up to stop him, "One sec, James. When we finish this call tonight, I want those who saw bats to write down their descriptions. Do not collaborate, just what YOU saw, please. Email those over tonight. Noelle and Haydee will go to work on them." He acknowledged James, "Okay, go ahead.'

Tony said, "If I may let me give you Alice's and the kid's report first. As you know, the twins were moved to the same school as the other three persons of interest, Cash, Lily, and Beth. James is sub-bing in a sixth-grade class, and Alex is in that same class. Audrey is in a third-grade class, and Alice is an office aide to a lady they call Sadie."

"Do we know why they were moved? I mean, we have some speculation," said James.

"Problems at the other school were all we were told," said Gunner.

Tony continued, "Alice met the twins, Sean and Sheena, almost immediately, and their mother, Joanne."

"They are mean and rude," Audrey's voice came from off-screen.

Tony continued, "Audrey's correct. Everyone has the same opinion about the twins. Alice took Alex and Audrey to a birthday party for them, and the twins never showed up, nor their parents."

He looked at Alice, and she continued, "There were at least fifty kids there, and the nannie, Natalie, but no birthday kids. I did learn that Mr. Branson, the kid's dad, has an older son, no idea how he ties into anything or if he does. But we are talking about an extremely wealthy family and two spoiled, neglected kids."

Tony looked at her, "Neglected. You never mentioned that."

Alice said, "It makes me sad. Sheena has loneliness in her eyes. I saw that on the first day. They have everything a kid could want but seem to lack love."

Tony's nonchalant look made Gunner chuckle, and Tony said, "Leave it to a mom. I don't think her kids would agree."

Alex poked his head into the camera, "You got that right. They are the worst kids ever."

Alice sighed, but then she went a different direction, "We were leaving the party, and as I pulled out of the driveway, a swarm of bats flew right at the windshield. It scared all of us. I slammed on the breaks, and then they flew away, together, like a black cloud," she shuddered, "It was awful."

"Could you describe them?" asked Gunner.

Alice looked at him quizzically, "They were bats."

Gunner's squinted, and he twisted his mouth, "Okay. So, James. You had an experience like none of yours, correct?"

James nodded, "I was at the hotel; I had just met with Ilene in the lobby, went back to the room to change to meet Alice and the kids for dinner, and then headed for the elevator. I heard the most deafening screeching along with the wind that seemed to come from the window at the end of the hall. Coming at me was a bat the size of a man. I kid you not; its wings hit the walls on both sides of the hall. It flew right at me, but then it stood up, which made no sense, but it did. The screeching suddenly stopped, and the stupid thing just vanished. Gone! It was the craziest and probably the most frightening experience I've ever had."

James put his arm around Alice. "I called Tony; he was on the phone with Alice. He heard what happened to her and told her to return to the hotel. I didn't want them to, but Tony insisted. It's been fine since we got here."

Gunner looked thoughtful and said, "Okay, good work, everyone. James and Alice, I need you and the kids to do the same thing. Your own personal description of the bats, or bat in James's case, that you saw, and email it over."

"We'll keep researching here on our end; let's collaborate in two days unless something comes up and you want to meet sooner. Craig, Char, Ilene, and Tony, we're going to a secured line; the rest of you, good night."

The screen went black.

Gunner told Noelle and Haydee, "I'd like you two to go over to the main house with your grandma right now; I'll explain later. Take the Hummer."

The girls turned off their computers and left.

⊶ 22 ⊷

SURPRISE

"Wow, I'VE NEVER DRIVEN this before. This will be fun." Haydee started the Hummer "What do you think that was all about?"

Noelle closed her door, "Do you mean the bats or Gunner suddenly closing the meeting?"

"All of it, not so much Gunner; that's his style. I guess I mean the secured line. Do we need a seatbelt? We're going five miles an hour in the sand on a deserted beach…"

"I'm not wearing mine, so don't kill us."

Haydee rolled her eyes, "Why isn't it beeping to tell us we're not wearing them?"

"Uncle Biron disconnected it."

"Oh."

Noelle sighed, "I don't know what to think. I wish I knew our role in all of this."

Haydee changed the subject, "It's so beautiful here." She drove along the edge of the sand as close to the water as she dared until the road turned into the tropical forest part of the island. "Do you ever just want to pinch yourself? You know that we're even here?"

"I know. When I really think about all that's happened the last eight years, I can't believe it. That first year when grandma didn't know. So crazy."

"And now we are all over the country taking down—whatever." Haydee took a deep breath and then let it escape slowly. "It's exciting, but it's scary.

The Hummer wound down the narrow road, shrouded in palm trees and thick, lush greenery. The main house on Mayajaal came into view.

"Hey, do you hear a helicopter?" Haydee rolled the Hummer to a stop.

"Yeah, wonder who that is?"

"Maybe someone coming back early from the mission."

"I don't think they've had time to get home; we just talked to them half an hour ago."

"Oh yeah, good point; let's get to the house; it sounds like it's landing nearby," said Noelle.

Haydee pulled to a stop just as Grandma stepped out on the porch. "Girls, hi! I didn't know you were coming."

Noelle jumped out, "Gunner sent us. We thought you needed us."

Grandma pulled them both into a hug. "I always need my girls."

They heard the helicopter lift off.

"Who is that? Are you girls expecting someone?"

They both shook their heads.

"Hey!"

Noelle knew that voice immediately and she whirled around, "Samual!"

Her brother emerged from the palm trees, followed close behind by Grant.

"Grant!" Haydee threw her arms around her cousin.

Grandma hugged them all at the same time. "What a nice surprise! Do your parents know you're here?"

"No," said Grant, "Some guy named Gunner does, though."

"Oh yeah, Gunner. He's in charge of our missions right now," said Haydee. "You'll like him."

"Why are you two here? Aren't you supposed to be on a ship or flying somewhere?" asked Noelle.

"We don't know exactly how this came down the pipeline, but we were both promoted and sent home," said Samual.

"Did Gunner request that?" asked Grandma.

Samual and Grant exchanged a quick glance, and then Grant said, "We don't know. It was all hush hush for both of us."

"How long are you staying?"

"We don't have any idea, Grandma," said Samual. "I was at sea; they brought me in with little details."

"Same here," said Grant, "I just got back from Saudi Arabia a couple of weeks ago."

Grandma linked arms with them both, "Well, now you're here, so we'll enjoy you while you are. Let's go inside and find something to eat. You all must be hungry."

❧ 23 ❧

Evaluate

Sulo sat on the edge of his seat; he leaned forward, his elbows on his knees, his hands folded together in front of him. His expression was more serious than Erikki had ever seen, which was saying something since Erikki had never seen Sulo smile.

But today, the feeling was tense and foreboding, and the air felt heavy. Murmurings throughout the room were about the same subject—why was Sulo not sitting in the commander chair as he always had?

Team members sent to America currently serve in different branches of the Norwegian military. Erikki and Alpo were both privates first class in the Norwegian Army.

This was about to change.

A sergeant first class stepped up in front of the room; the entire company immediately stood at attention and saluted when the Chief of Defence entered, went directly to the podium, and stood between Sulo and Torsten.

The chief saluted and then motioned for them all to be seated. However, he remained standing.

"This is an unusual circumstance that I have been called to attend this morning. Your elders, Sulo and Torsten, have a great concern. They have spent considerable time explaining to me the

96

worries of this menace now in America, but that originated here, centuries ago."

"I agree with them that this must be stopped. Rannug Relhi left Norway, traveling to America, bestowing the superpowers on his progenitors. His father, Elo, should have exercised more control over his son." He paused for several seconds.

"Although the public was not made aware of the Relhi family's unusual supernatural powers, our government has had access to them for centuries, so the superpowers themselves are not the issue, just the opposite. However, now that this branch of the Relhi family is no longer within the boundaries and jurisdiction of this country, they must be eradicated."

"The members of the Relhi family, although well respected in the past, have gone rogue, posing a threat to the protected anonymity of these powers that have existed in Norwegian history for centuries."

The chief looked at Sulo and asked, "How many young people now have these powers?"

Sulo sighed and glanced at Torsten, "Seventeen, not including their grandmother, so eighteen in all."

Torsten added, "Rannug Relhi is not the first to leave Norway, but he is the first to take these powers beyond our borders and to America of all places," he scoffed, "Who knows to what extent they will abuse them."

The chief nodded but asked, "Does the grandmother have a name?"

"Dede Relhi. She was christened Deodora. She doesn't have a superhuman power; she *apparently* has a supernatural connection with spirits."

The chief looked thoughtful but then turned back to the company and said, "My purpose here today is to commission a temporary special forces team. All of you."

This was completely unexpected. Erikki and Alpo glanced anxiously at each other as a low murmur rolled through the crowd of young men and women.

The chief raised his hand, and the room became silent again, "This is not to say you are going to kill them. Your mission is to deactivate their power. Stop them." He turned to Sulo and nodded, then sat in the commander's chair.

Sulo stood, "One of the reasons this group was selected for this mission is your ability to shape shift. We chose bats, and before you left, you were given the ability to incapacitate a subject with the ultrasonic sting from your wings. This is still the case; we added a little more." He turned the time over to Torsten.

The screen behind the podium lit up, and an image of a bat appeared. With a laser, Torsten pointed to the tiny lights on the underside of the wings. This is Rancon; its beam can be lethal, but its effect is a little different in his case. In addition, now Rancon will emit a numbing beam that will last only fifteen seconds. Your subject will be helpless, giving you time to direct Rancon to its target. Which is only one place," the image of the bat changed to a man, and Torsten pointed the laser again.

"Here, in the center of the forehead, this is the only place it is effective. Our goal is not to kill the subjects but to deactivate their power."

Torsten looked at Sulo, who added, "It is important that you remember that you're here because you have already suffered death; therefore, immortal. You cannot be killed. Injured, yes, but you will not die."

The image on the screen changed again. This time, it was Anders, the century-old captain of the Norwegian Army.

"You all know Anders; you will report to him by 0500 hours tomorrow morning, where you will again meet with Heimdall, who will administer the numbing potion to your wings. This is a process, so be patient. Once completed, we will all reconvene in this room where you failed," he paused, "Previous missions will be evaluated, and your new mission and teams will be assigned. We expect to have you back in America within a week."

Sulo turned to the chief and said, "Thank you for blessing and commissioning these special forces for Rancon."

The chief nodded and stood, and the company stood, too. They saluted, and the leader left the podium. Once he left the room, Torsten said to the company, "Dismissed."

Erikki and Alpo started for the door, and Linnea and Dan caught up to them. The four walked towards the diner.

"This is unbelievable; special forces?" Dan was so excited he could barely get the words out.

"It is exciting to be a part of it for sure," said Alpo, "I was a little disappointed though."

"That we can't kill them?" Erikki didn't wait for an answer, "I know, me too, but at least they won't be using those superpowers anymore."

Linnea said, "I was surprised at how expert and well-developed their powers are. They must have had some serious training to fine-tune them like that. When we attempted the attack on the two children with their mother, that little girl in the back, whether she realized it or not, threw up some sort of shield, and we could not penetrate it."

"What do you mean knew it or not? Of course, she knew it," said Dan.

"I don't think so, she looked up and screamed. That's what I mean by fine-tuned. It seems so natural like they don't have to force it."

Erikki sighed, "Maybe. I wonder if they will have us go in the groups again and try to take them while they are separated and trying to get the woman—what is her name?"

"Geist, yeah, that's a code name for her. Geist,' said Alpo.

"They have their hands full there," said Dan.

The four took seats in a booth and ordered sandwiches.

"I was disappointed that we didn't even get to use Rancon. I hope it works. Did *anyone* get the chance to use it?" asked Linnea.

"If they did, no one mentioned it. I'm sure we'll find out in the briefing," said Erikki.

"Yeah, most likely," said Dan.

"Are you guys scared?" asked Linnea.

"A little," said Alpo.

"But we can't be killed, right?"

Alpo turned to his over-enthusiastic friend, "No, Erikki, but the consequences can be severe. I would prefer to live the next thousand years with all my limbs and senses."

Erikki looked out the window, "Yeah, I guess I'm a little scared."

～ 24 ～

SECURED LINE

GUNNER SKIPPED PLEASANTRIES and got straight to business. "I have had Noelle and Haydee researching bats for a week—they can't find any particular bat that is native to the states we are operating in, as well as Egypt. They had to have been transplanted. I put the other two cousins on surveillance. Both can hear thoughts, so I sent them to Norway. I have a suspicion this whole bat thing started there."

"That would make sense," said Char, "Isn't that where the crow came from in the beginning?"

"Exactly. What they found…"

"Who are they?" asked Tony.

"Oh, sorry," said Gunner, "The two cousins in the military. Grant Air Force and Samual Navy. We got them promoted in rank so they could be sent on an official mission to Norway. To clarify a little, Samual is Richard's son, and Grant is Janae's."

"Okay, thanks." Said Tony.

Gunner smiled, "Sorry, a lot on my mind," he continued, "They're back now. I met with them yesterday in Belize to get a full report of their findings. It's more than I ever imagined, but we'll get details when everyone returns here. In the meantime, we must alert our teams that the bats are a clear danger to this mission. We are stepping up our operation; get in and get out."

"You mean in the schools?" asked Ilene.

"Yes, this woman, Geist, is one cog in a huge machine, but if we can get to her, we can stop the progression, at least in the schools. I hope. I don't think we can eradicate the colleges yet, maybe, but I suspect that is a much bigger web."

"So, what's the plan?" asked Craig. "There are a lot of moving parts here."

Gunner sighed, "That's an understatement."

"Let's start with you, Ilene. The activity there seems to be the lowest key so far."

"You mean boring?" laughed Ilene.

"Yes, that. What we know so far is that Tommy has a brother, Clay, who he has invited to a gaming party to meet Brighton; Gracie has a cousin, Vicki, who doesn't seem to be too involved; and Gracie has a friend named Oliver, who might be the same Oliver the other kids are talking about? Do I have that right so far?"

"Yes," said Ilene. "The party is taking place this coming Wednesday after school."

"So, in five days."

Ilene nodded, "Yes."

Gunner said, "Okay, Tony, you have the most sensitive situation, I realize that. Dealing with little kids is not easy. However, the twin's stepbrother may be the connection we're looking for."

Tony looked surprised, "Oliver?"

"Yes, I can't explain why I think that; call it a gut feeling. But that name has come up all too often. I'm not sure how much involvement the twins have, but I know another girl, Lily, a third grader, with a gaming club."

"A third grader?" said Craig.

"I know, right. There seems to be a connection through the studio where the little girl dances."

"Is this Lily or Beth?" asked Tony.

"Lily. Beth and Cash seem, at this point, to maybe have been in the wrong place at the wrong time. So, for now, we concentrate on Lily. We're thinking the twin's nanny, Natalie, may be able to get us a connection to this Oliver."

Tony said, "Okay, boss."

Gunner ignored him and went onto Craig, "So we have Marla and Tracee, the cheerleaders, Lance and Brett, the football players, and again another friend to Oliver, Tracee. Am I missing anyone?"

"No," said Craig. "The biggest obstacle we have is that Zion is on his own. Nate is not at the school, and Katie is a teacher, but at the other end of the building from where Zion is most of the time."

"I think we figured out that dilemma, but you're right; we should have sent someone else in with Zion. We thought of sending Haydee or Noelle in, but Zion has made some great connections—I think adding more bodies will complicate things. I'll come back to that in a second."

Gunner continued, "Char, talk about a tangled web up there in San Jose."

Char sighed, "It is, but I've been thinking, wouldn't it be because this is where Geist is located? That would make total sense. Her biggest influence is going to be right where she is."

"Can't disagree with that, "Gunner raised his brows and shook his head slightly, "Let's look at this. Stop me if you get lost in the menagerie. According to Mack, we have Mel, Bryan, and Britt, who is a brat. We have squirrely little Steve, who seems to be the head honcho in the gaming community there. Then Mr. Cutler, or Jon, runs the computer lab and is apparently not Keeper. No, Oliver, correct so far?"

"Correct," said Char.

"Okay, oh, and by the way, Ilene, I forgot to mention Ember Hunter, the vice principal in Iowa. Brighton met her. She seems to be a non-figure now, but we'll see." Gunner looked away from his notes on the screen.

Ilene asked, "Nonfigure?"

"Not important. We think."

"Okay, that covers it. Now, let's narrow it down. This is what we've found. Our Mr. Oliver Branson is key here. When I say here, I mean with the schools. The chain of command appears to be Geist, then Steve, who works directly with her. Steve's gopher is Britt; she is basically a recruiter. Which is probably why she was so resistant to Ava and Micah. She didn't have a direct connection with them, which cut into her profits. Next, Cutler is the central liaison for this school. He basically provides the workshop. Now let's go to Oliver, this, my friend, is Keeper. We put two special agents in the field to do surveillance, and he is everywhere."

Gunner brought some photos up on the screen. "Oliver Branson, son of multi-millionaire oil tycoon Gordon Branson, stepson of Joanne, and stepbrother to Sheena and Sean."

The entire family's faces appeared on the screen. "The twins are collateral damage. That will be covered later." The family disappeared, leaving only Oliver on the screen.

"Oliver is the ringleader, recruiter, whatever you want to call him, and we found a direct link to each of the groups your teams are working on."

"Ilene, Oliver is Gracie's friend, but our innocent bystander, Vicki, is his direct contact at that school."

"Craig, again, the one who seems so aloof. Brett is the direct contact with Oliver."

"Tony, the obvious connection here would be Natalie, the nanny, but it's Joanne, the kid's mother."

"Char, in your case, Oliver and Cutler work hand in hand. Their job is to bring in the Vickie's, Brett's, and Britts from other schools."

"How in the world Joanne got involved and included her kids is another story altogether, and quite honestly, the most irritating to me."

"Here's the clincher: in the past month, Oliver and Cutler have recruited," more pictures popped up on the screen, "Brandi in New Mexico, Chad in Montana, Marsha in Kansas, and Randy in Maryland. Those are the ones we know about."

Gunner added the pictures of Britt, Brett, Vickie, and Cutler, with Oliver in the middle and Geist just above him.

"Your assignments are tailored to your unique situations. I emailed each of you your orders—the files are encrypted—the passwords will be given to you when we disconnect this call. Praxis is going to come to the forefront and fast."

Almost as an afterthought, Gunner said, "I have information on the bats for you, but it's not pertinent to this operation. We'll meet on Sunday evening and go over it together. I wanted to meet with Samual and Grant, and they just returned. Their parents will arrive later today, and they haven't seen their boys for some time. Get together with your teams today and review the new outlines so they are ready to run on Monday. Questions?"

Silence.

"Okay, that's it then."

The screen went black.

ॐ 25 ॐ

REVISED MISSIONS

EACH MEMBER of the special forces team had to meet with Heimdall for the process of adding the numbing effect to the bat wings. Each person had to morph into a bat for several minutes. Some took as long as half an hour.

It had been a long day already, and they hadn't even me with their team leaders yet.

Linnea was the last of the four friends to exit Heimdall's lab. "That was not fun."

"It was painful," said Dan.

"It was but I can't feel it anymore, can any of you?" asked Erikki.

They all shook their heads. They were among the last to arrive at the hall where they were being assigned teams and duties in preparation to leave for America. Members of the special forces were not assigned uniforms for this mission. They were divided into five teams of eight, the ones who were not assigned to one of the Nessumsar groups would be in America on call, in an undisclosed location.

Mission specifics were outlined for each circumstance, and names were assigned. Team one Maize; team two Harvest; team three Littoral; team four Interval; team five Shoal.

Alpo, Erikki, Dan, and Linnea were disappointed that they were assigned to different teams.

Alpo to California, Dan to Florida, Linnea to Iowa, and Erikki to Belize. They met with their team leaders, however not much instruction was given at this point. They were told that when the plane landed in New York, they would board flights for their state and then rent a car from there to their destination.

Team Shoal, going to Belize, would fly directly there from Norway.

The mood in the hall was both excitement and uncertainty. Each member of the special forces knew they had been handpicked for this mission. Having a better understanding of the highly skilled Nessumsar family, caused feelings of both honor, and fear.

∽ 26 ∽

Game On

At 4:00 on Wednesday afternoon, Kitana dropped Lock off at Gracie's house for the gaming party. Tommy and his brother Clay were already there. Vicki had spent the night with her cousin, and Brighton arrived in an Uber.

Tommy and Clay stood on the front sidewalk when the Uber pulled up. "My parents are still at work," explained Brighton when she met with their surprised looks.

Tommy shrugged, "Okay, this is my brother, Clay, this is Brighton."

"Hi!" Brighton greeted him enthusiastically.

"Nice to meet you," said Tommy.

Brighton thought he seemed a little shy.

Tommy opened the door, "Well, let's go in; Gracie has food."

Brighton laughed, "Uh, one sec," but then she heard through her ear mic, "I can hear you, Brighton, loud and clear."

She was relieved to hear Ilene's voice and followed the two boys into the house. Before closing the door, she glanced over her shoulder. Kitana was on the front steps, but her appearance was brief, and then she disappeared.

Brighton stepped into the living room. Lock was seated next to Vicki, and Gracie placed a platter of cheese and crackers on the coffee table in the center of the room. She greeted them, "Hi, you guys! I brought enough chairs in for all of you, and if you need power, there are Surge protectors behind each chair."

Brighton took a chair across from Lock, and Tommy and Clay took the two chairs next to her. That left a chair for Gracie and one empty chair.

Tommy introduced Lock to Clay and Brighton.

Gracie had gone back to the kitchen. When she came back in, Tommy asked, "Who's the other chair for?"

Gracie shrugged, "I'm not sure. Vicki said she may have a friend coming." She turned to her cousin, "Right?"

Vicki nodded but seemed a little uncomfortable. "I'm not sure when; let's just get started."

Gracie sat next to Lock and said, "Okay, you should all have access to Praxis now, but before we start, put on your headset."

Lock was intrigued by Vicki's seeming knowledge of the gaming system. She seemed aloof most of the time and did not engage in conversation.

Gracie said, "Alexa, lights out."

The virtual assistant promptly turned the lights off. Closed blinds blocked the late afternoon sun.

Lock waited for the screen to load the new game, but as he did, he noticed a background sound coming through the headphones. There seemed to be an underlying tone; he couldn't distinguish it. He looked over at Kitana, who he knew was sitting on the sofa behind Brighton. He could barely hear Ilene through this earpiece.

"I can't hear it, but Kitana sent me a text. She can hear it and is patched into Frank's computer in California. She is sending it to us; we'll try to isolate it."

PRAXIS loaded on Lock's screen. He glanced at Brighton. The computer screen lit her face as it did everyone else's. She looked up directly at Lock and then looked back down.

The screen and the voice through the headsets said, *Welcome to Praxis, a journey of learning and exploration; learn how to get what you want when you want it while remaining anonymous.'*

The game started with obstacles to challenge a player's ability to escape different situations. Lock didn't find them very difficult. He made it to the next level. He glanced over at Brighton; she seemed to be struggling. He knew she wasn't into gaming at all.

The music and subtle tone were now becoming soothing rather than irritating, and Lock concentrated more on the screen than the music.

The next level was a series of locks and safes. The player's challenge was dismantling or otherwise gaining entry to each one. It was a little more challenging but not complex for Lock. Through the headset, he heard, almost in the background, *'Where do you want to go? What would you like to do? To become? To see? To experience? To be, to be, to be...'*

The voice paused and then repeated the exact words over and over.

He looked around the room; Gracie and Brighton looked a little stressed; he suspected they were still stuck on level one. But Tommy, Clay, and especially Vicki visibly enjoyed the new game.

Lock breezed through the following seven levels; he was surprised when level ten started, and the first thing that appeared was a dollar sign in the center of the screen. It seemed to freeze, then right under it, spelled out slowly the words, *'Why don't we make this worth your time...'*

"Are you seeing this?" he whispered into his mic.

"Yes." That was all Ilene said.

"What about Brighton?"

Ilene chuckled, "She is only on level two."

Lock looked over at Brighton. He knew she was privy to this conversation. She glanced up and scowled.

Observing, Frank spoke into his mic transmitting to Char. "Wow, they make this easy. Clever ways to steal. Lock has racked up fifty dollars already. He's a little too good at this."

Level Ten ended, and Lock was surprised to see a series of blinking dots scrolling across the screen. After a full minute, the words... *'we want to send you your money. Enter your social security number'...* then it was gone.

At the same time, the female voice through the headset said, *if you don't have a bank account, we can arrange for a pickup.*

Immediately, the screen flashed TOTAL EARNINGS $50 in giant letters, and then it immediately switched back to levels.

"Hey, did anyone else earn money on level ten?" he asked the group.

"I did," Tommy flipped his hand up quickly, "Twenty bucks."

"Dude, you're not as good a thief as me." Lock laughed.

A wry smile crossed Vicki's face, "I'm at a hundred and five."

"What? What did I miss?" asked Lock.

"Did you complete all the tasks?" asked Vicki.

"Wait, how do you know so much about this game?" Gracie demanded of her cousin. "You never even seemed interested."

Vicki cocked her head, "Things are not always as they seem." She put her laptop down and walked over to Lock. "Go back to level ten for a second."

Lock used his controller to get him back to the beginning of level ten. Brighton and Tommy had joined them by peering over his shoulder.

The game indicated Lock had finished, so Vicki took his controller and got him back to the last challenge. On the right of the screen was a tiny safe with the words *Over here* on the front.

"You missed that," said Vicki.

"I didn't even see it."

"It was there. It pops up after you complete the second to last challenge, so you won't leave the screen without seeing it."

"What does it say?"

"Open it."

Lock looked up at Vicki, took his controller, and clicked on the safe. The door slowly opened, but there was nothing in it.

"There…"

"Just wait," said Vicki.

Quietly but now building, Lock heard from the headset, *'Praxis to be me, to me, to me, to me…'*

He thought he heard something else, more subtle. He couldn't quite make it out.

Then he heard Kitana, "It is saying 'Vickeee.' *'Listen to me'*...it sounds like *'Vickeee'.*"

Startled, Lock looked up at Vicki. She obviously thought he figured it out and said, "Interested?"

Lock nodded. "Duh."

Vicki laughed, and Gracie flipped on the lights.

"Well, obviously, the only ones who get this game are Tommy, Lock, and, strangely enough, my cousin." She sighed, "Who wants ice cream?" She turned to Vicki, "By the way, where is your friend?"

"He texted me; he couldn't make it this time."

"Oh, too bad. Maybe he could have won money, too."

"It's one thing for the computer to say we won; the question is, how do we get the dough?"

Clay laughed at his brother, "Dough? Are we a gangster now?"

Tommy grinned at Lock, "Kind of feels like it."

Lock started to agree, but Kitana's voice came through the headset, "You are."

He smiled, but he knew Brighton heard it when she laughed out loud. Everyone looked at her, but she just raised her eyebrows.

Kitana said, "You are so bad at being quiet." Locked looked for Brighton's reaction. It appeared she was scowling at an empty sofa, but Lock knew Kitana was sitting there.

Lock grabbed a soda from the cooler by the front door and walked outside.

Vicki followed him.

Tommy was already sitting on the step, and Lock joined him.

"Get as much information as you can," Kitana came through the headset, but Frank interrupted her, "Address, location."

Lock yawned and whispered, "You guys are giving me a headache."

"Do you have a headache?" asked Vicki.

"Uh, no. No, I was just yawning."

"How can we make more money at this game?" asked Tommy.

Vicki narrowed her eyes, "Are you sure you're interested? There is big money to be had."

"Praxis?" asked Tommy.

She nodded, "Yes, that too. But there are other ways…" she paused, "Text me your number, Lock, I have yours, Tommy. I'll get back to both of you. Right now, I think Gracie is annoyed with me."

Gracie popped her head out the front door, "Are you guys coming in for ice cream? I have banana splits!"

"Coming!" they said in unison.

Dan and his teammate Astrid clung to a branch in the tree in Gracie's front yard. They chose to be in bat form to be closer to their persons of interest and use their keen sense of hearing to pick up conversations.

"What do you think?"

Dan took a deep breath and slowly let his chest expand. "I think we need to watch the cousins for when they are alone, the three of them, I mean."

"Alone would be better."

"It's hard to catch the two girls; they're capable of disappearing."

"What about him?"

"Shapeshifter."

Astrid rolled her eyes, "Oh great."

❧ 27 ❧

CHEETAH

CHAPARRAL WON the game again, but it was a close call this time. They played Highland High and only pulled ahead with an extra point. It looked like Highland had it when they scored, but they missed the kick.

Lance took the ball over the goal line for the extra point after their touchdown in the last thirty seconds of the game.

Chaparral had the kickoff; Highland fumbled, but their quarterback recovered the ball, and he charged down the field.

It caught Chaparral's players off guard, and the quarterback made a clean break down the center, weaving unscathed through the opposing team.

Attempted tackles failed, while well-placed blocks succeeded.

Zion was on the opposite side of the field when he realized they were about to lose the game. He started to run, but then he took a deep breath, blew it out, and surged forward. Zion was running so fast that no one could catch him.

Spectators on both sides jumped to their feet. Chaparrals fans exploded into cheers while Highlands stood speechless.

Within a couple of feet of the quarterback and another three feet to the goal, Zion leaped through the air, wrapping his arms around the player's waist, both plowing into the turf.

The clock ran out, and Chaparral had another win under their belt.

The dismayed quarterback jumped up to face Zion, "What the…? Where did you come from?!"

Zion grinned, "Oh, I'm from California."

The quarterback scowled, turned, and jogged toward his teammates, staring in awe at Zion.

Zion heard him yell, "What's the matter? Haven't you ever seen anyone run before?"

By this time, Zion's teammates were all over him, equally as stunned by Zion's fast run as the other team.

Zion blew it off and walked across the field toward the field house. He and Lance lagged behind the group, and Brett dropped back to join them.

"Holy Moley, Zion. What was that?" said Brett.

"Running." Zion pulled off his helmet and grinned.

"Running? It's more like flying. Did your feet even touch the ground? Dude, how tall are you?"

"Six-two," said Zion. "And it was just running."

"Could have fooled me," Lance shook his head.

"You won the game with the extra point you ran," said Zion.

Lance laughed, "But you saved the win by becoming a cheetah! Geez, unbelievable."

"We won; it takes a whole team." Zion looked up to see the coach heading in his direction. He started to take off his cleats and noticed the coach was stopped by the school news reporter.

"So, before he gets here and you sign autographs, Oliver was impressed with your gaming skills after the game at Tracee's the other day. He would like you to come again." Brett looked past Zion, "You too, Lance."

"Thanks for the afterthought."

"No way, it's not like that. But Zion is good at this, and Oliver is looking for strong players for tournaments. He has a new game he wants to get a team together to learn. He thought you, you guys, might be interested."

Zion put his cleats on the floor.

If they only knew.

Zion stood when the coach approached, "Coach?" He glanced at Brett, "Sure, I'll come." He looked at Lance, "We'll both come."

Alpo and his teammate, Emil, watched the game from Highlands stands and were equally shocked to see Zion's gazelle run.

"Whew, that guy is good," said Emil.

"How fast do you think he was running?" asked Alpo.

"I'm not sure, but we can fly."

"Only about twenty-five miles an hour. He was running faster than that."

"Well, at least we know." Suddenly startled, Emil looked past Alpo, "That girl wasn't there one second ago."

Alpo whirled around, "What, girl?" But he immediately recognized the girl he had pushed into the bushes.

Katie glanced up at them; she didn't look away.

"That's one of the Nessumsar family."

Alpo and Katie locked eyes, and then Katie was gone.

Alpo and Emil stared at the place where she had been. Finally, they started down the bleachers. When they reached the track, Alpo noticed the girl again, going through the gate into the parking lot. Now she was walking with a man.

Katie glanced over her shoulder, looking directly at Alpo just before she and Nate vanished.

"They recognized me."

"They?" asked Emil quizzically.

"Yeah, she was at the house the other night. I pushed her into the bushes, but then she vanished."

"Okay, who are they?"

"Oh, I don't know who the guy is, but they both can become invisible."

Emil raised his eyebrows, "Great, one we can't catch and two that disappear. This should be fun."

∽ 28 ∾

SIR STEVE

MACK WAS SURPRISED to find the Computer Lab door locked when he showed up for his appointment with Mr. Cutler.

He checked his phone, "Nope, right day and time." He didn't have a phone number to contact Mr. Cutler, so he stood there trying to figure out what to do.

He thought he saw someone move toward the back of the lab through the glass door, but cabinets and a partial wall obstructed his view.

"Mack?"

Mack spun around, "Oh, Mr. Cutler, I thought you forgot about our appointment today."

Mr. Cutler smacked his forehead with his palm, "Was that today?"

"Yes, do you still have time?"

Mr. Cutler put his key in the door but didn't open it. "I don't today, Mack. Something has come up, but please call me Jon. We are colleagues."

"Okay, Jon. Sorry to hear that, though. I was looking forward to this."

Jon glanced through the door, and Mack said, "I thought I saw someone in there, maybe not."

"Uh, no. There's no one here today. Can you excuse me, Mack? I really must get to some pressing matters."

"Oh, sure, sorry. Maybe next week."

"Yes, that would work." Jon opened the door only wide enough for him to get through, and then he closed it, locking it from the inside.

Mack turned and walked down the hallway. "Did you hear all of that?"

Char responded through Mack's earpiece, "I did."

"I thought you said Ava and Micah were meeting at the computer lab today."

"They are, they're already there. Hold on…"

"Ava said they were told to come to the back entrance to the lab; it's down a hallway in the back of the auditorium."

"Hey, Mr…"

Mack looked up from his phone. Mel and Bryan were coming down the hall.

"Mack, just call me Mack. I'm used to Coach Mack because I usually coach swimming. Still at school, I, see?"

"We both had detention," said Bryan.

Mel furrowed his brow, "I didn't have detention; you did. I did homework waiting to give you a ride home."

Mack laughed, "I guess it could be considered one and the same."

Mel shrugged, "Pretty much."

"Are you looking for Mr. Cutler?" asked Bryan.

"I was, but I just spoke to him. He had something come up, so we couldn't meet today."

"Oh yeah, he mentioned earlier today that he had something important right after school."

"Hmm, well, I'll get with him another time. Have a good one." Mack walked away and, when out of earshot of the boys, whispered to Char, "Ask Ava or Micah to let you know when, or if, Mel and Bryan show up. I just saw them in the hall over here."

Mack rounded the corner and stopped, looking back toward the computer lab. The boys were gone. He was trying to figure out what to do when Char said, "Apparently, Spencer is inside the lab with the girls."

"Great, okay, I'll head out to the parking lot and wait."

"Mack?"

"I'm here."

"Spencer said to come back to the door."

"The lab?"

"Yes, he wants to know if you think you can shapeshift into a bug," Char chuckled.

"A bug? Is he serious?"

"I guess. That's what he said."

Mack headed back to the lab, "Well, I can't, geez."

A bug, what's wrong with…wait, maybe…

Mack stopped where he was and looked around. He was getting better at changing shapes. He closed his eyes and almost instantly began shrinking. When he opened them again, everything was huge. He ran across the hall—it took him longer this time. When he reached the computer lab, he stopped.

Oh, whoops, I can't see in the window.

He heard the doorknob turning and backed away quickly.

He could not see anyone at the door.

"Mack?"

"Spencer?"

"Where are you?"

"I'm right here, down here."

"A mouse?" Spencer started laughing and began to materialize.

"Yes. And quit laughing. I can see you."

Spencer stopped abruptly, "Didn't know that would happen, hurry and get in here."

Mack scurried through the door.

"Are you in?" Mack was surprised he could still hear Char. Did his earpiece shrink too?

"He's in, and what a cute mouse he is," said Spencer.

Char laughed, "I'm quite sure I have completely lost it. I am talking to an invisible man and a mouse!"

"And hurting my ears," said Mack.

"Shh," Spencer whispered.

They came around a partition into the lab; Britt stood at the front of the group. Mel. Bryan, Ava. Micah, Mr. Cutler, and someone Mack didn't recognize were seated on the stools in front of the computer stations.

They were all wearing headsets, and Britt was explaining something to them. She had a mic on her headset; the sound was obviously going into the headset because he couldn't hear anything she was saying.

"We can't hear her," whispered Spencer.

"I can. Frank is here and patched in. He said she is giving them instructions on how to get past level ten and into the cyber portion of the game."

"Praxis?" asked Mack.

"Yes. Frank said Lock got to level ten but no further. That's where they stopped."

"Maybe these kids are more experienced."

"That's what we're thinking."

"Maybe Micah, but not Ava," said Spencer.

"True." Char continued, "Apparently, Mel, Bryan, and Micah made nearly two hundred dollars each in level ten. Frank is saying Mack only got to fifty and is more experienced in gaming than Micah."

"I don't think he is," said Mack. "They both play a lot."

"How is Ava?" asked Spencer.

"Poor," said Char. "Just kidding."

"You do have a sense of humor," said Mack.

"Don't push it."

"So, what's happening? Wait, never mind, they're taking off their headsets," said Spencer.

Britt said, "What do you think, Mr. Cutler? Are we ready?"

"I think so."

Jon turned to the kid Mack didn't recognize, but now that he had time to study him from his mouse position, he guessed he was squirrely Steve, as Gunner described. His guess was correct.

"Are they ready, Steve?"

Steve was typing something on an iPad. He glanced over at Jon, "More than ready. I'm getting confirmation on the time and place."

For what?

Curiosity was killing Mack.

When Steve spoke, everyone, without standing, came to attention. Mack was surprised that this little, barely five-foot kid ordered these big, burly boys around. But he did; that was obvious.

Steve spun around on his stool. "This is a big preliminary game; we are trying to get the best players we put together in one spot. Leave your phone numbers with Britt so we can text you the details."

Mack knew this had been an issue already with Lock. So, Ilene requested their contacts equip the kids with burner phones, but they could not text out; they could only answer if a text came in. And they couldn't receive or make calls.

"That's it?" Mel stood, "I need to get home."

Steve looked annoyed, "Sorry to hold you up while I show you how to make a fortune."

Mel stopped; he rolled his eyes in the other kids' direction but turned around to Steve, "Thank you, Sir Steve."

Steve glared at Mel, "I told you not to call me that."

"Yeah, you did, but it fits you. You're, you know, the one in charge."

"Whatever. Make sure you all clean up the computer stations before you leave." He turned back to his computer and pulled his headset on.

Mel whispered to Ava and Micah, "You mean the horrible mess we made while sitting in one spot for over an hour without so much as a bottle of water? That guy bugs me."

Ava, Micah, and Bryan tried to conceal the smirks on their faces as they exited the lab through the back entrance.

Ava shrieked, "A mouse! I saw a mouse!" She turned and ran in the opposite direction, bumping into something solid, but nothing was there. She stopped abruptly.

"Ava, are you okay?" Mel grabbed her arm. "You look like you hit a wall, or…"

"The mouse scared me. Guess I just stopped fast."

Guess so.

Spencer rubbed his jaw. Ava's head hit him in the face.

Mack scurried to a corner before anyone stepped on him.

I have never seen a mouse back here," said Bryan.

First time for everything.

Mack ran past them as fast as he could.

"Me either, especially in the lab," said Mel. He opened the door to the auditorium, and they all went in.

Spencer hurried past them and into another hall.

Spencer and Mack met outside the school in the teacher's parking lot.

They laughed when Char said, "Are you two having fun?"

They both said, "Yeah."

They could hear her snicker. "Frank wants me to tell you that was some great information. Not that the two of you did anything."

"Hey, we came," said Spencer.

"We saw," Mack said with conviction.

"Well, good. Now, make sure you get that location. We have a feeling this is going to be something big."

"Got it," said Spencer.

"Over and out," said Mack.

"He's a smart alec," mumbled Char.

"We're still here. I heard that."

The mics went dead.

"I guess that's goodbye."

Mack rolled his eyes, "As good as it's going to get. Let's get some food before we go back to the hotel."

"Okay, we should be able to beat Char if she's at headquarters with Frank. Betos?"

"Sounds good. Are the girls taking an Uber?"

"Think so." Spencer climbed on the motorcycle, pulled on his helmet, and took off, and when a student opened the door to the Range Rover, Mack scurried in.

Mack looked up just in time to see two bats fly out of the school when a girl opened the door. She screamed and ran back inside.

Erikki and his team member, Nora, climbed into their SUV and sat quietly for a few minutes. They had been observing the bats from an open beam in the computer lab and did not want anyone to question two strange people in the school. They had to wait for someone to open the door so they could get out.

"Are you getting this? The Praxis game thing is happening all in one place?" Nora's eyes widened.

"It looks that way. We'll have to see if everyone else is getting the same info," said Erikki.

"That would be easier, though, if they're in one spot, right."

"I'm not sure; in this group alone, we have one who can become invisible and a shapeshifter."

"To a mouse." Nora sighed, "That's probably just one shape, though, huh?"

Erikki sighed, "This may be harder than we ever thought. There are seventeen of them."

⮜ 29 ⮞

THEY'RE JUST LITTLE KIDS

ALICE WALKED up the winding sidewalk and rang the overstated doorbell.

She waited several minutes, nothing, so she rang again.

Finally, the door opened. It was Joanne.

"Well, hi Alice. How are you?"

"Hi Joanne, I'm fine and sorry to barge in like this. I don't have your phone number. I tried the one on the registration card at school, but it was the wrong number."

"Really? I must have written it down wrong."

"I—we missed the kids at their birthday party."

Joanne nodded briefly, "Yeah, we didn't make it back in time. I, uh, enrolled Sheena in a dance class across town, and she, uh, had to do some auditions. We just didn't get out in time. I guess I could have sent Sean in an Uber, but I kind of hate to do that, you know? I know it's a kid, Uber, but you never know."

"Oh no, I would never send my kids in a taxi or anything like that. Alone."

There was an awkward silence before Joanne said, "Did you…?"

"Oh, sorry, Audrey thinks she lost her little princess bracelet, maybe in the jump house. It wasn't found by anyone, was it?"

Joanne sighed, "No, I'm so sorry. The jump house was deflated and picked up an hour after the party. I can look around, though, or I would happily buy her another one."

"Oh no, that isn't necessary. It was a gift from her grandmother; it wouldn't have the same meaning. I shouldn't have allowed her to wear it."

Alice suddenly felt foolish for even coming over, even though it was her orders and there never was a princess bracelet.

She started to walk away but then turned back; Joanne already had the door partially closed.

"Uh, where does Sheena dance? Aubrey would love to get back into it."

Joanne looked surprised, "Oh, it's called… I'm so embarrassed, I can't remember the studio's name; I know where it is; I can get to it."

Alice brushed the thought away with her hand, "No worries. I'm sorry to have bothered you about it. Anyway, thanks for inviting the kids to the party."

"Of course, bye now."

Joanne closed the door.

Alice was so stunned at the strange encounter that she stood motionless, trying to process what had just happened. She thought Joanne looked sad or depressed; she wasn't sure. She didn't appear to be the same put-together woman Alice met at school.

I did drop in unannounced. It's hardly a fair assessment.

She started to walk down the steps but stopped when she heard yelling from inside the house.

"I don't even know the woman; she works at the school!" screamed Joanne.

A male voice said, "She said her kids were at the party! You must know her; you invited her!"

"Sheena invited the little girl, and I included the boy. He is in Sean's class. They barely know each other!"

The male voice escalated; he sounded too young to be Joanne's husband.

"I told you; every contact is necessary!"

Alice felt embarrassed that she was privy to this conversation but couldn't walk away. Somehow, she felt it was important.

Suddenly, she realized she was standing right out in the open. She moved quickly away from the door to a nearby a bush where she was hidden from the street but still on the porch, so she could easily hear Joanne and the man.

"Who do you think you are?!" Joanne sounded like she was crying.

"You know who I am, *Mother*. I'm your ticket out of here, but not unless you fulfill our bargain."

"Oliver!"

Alice bristled.

"I'm tired! I just want to be a mother to my two children!"

"Two children?" he scoffed. "Well, you certainly haven't been one to me, that's for sure!"

"You've never let me; you've never wanted me to be!"

Oliver quieted now, "You know what? Just get the contacts I need. I'm under a lot of pressure, too. This game is happening next week, and I answer to Cutler and Steve, you know that." He almost mumbled, "And then Geist. I deliver, or I'm dead."

Joanne was crying more softly now, "I know. I'm sorry your father ever got you involved in this."

"Just keep using the little spoiled brats for contacts; you're good at that." He snickered, "They're getting pretty good at the game, too. Those subliminal suggestions we added for kids really work."

"Oliver, they're just little kids," Joanne whimpered.

Oliver said nothing.

Alice heard footsteps coming towards the door. She ran to the side of the house but then, in horror, realized her car was in the driveway. She had her purse in her hand and dropped it at her feet.

Why did I bring that?

Oliver opened the door but yelled back inside, "By the way, I got a text from another dance mom. Good job!"

He closed the door and started across the porch away from her toward the side of the house.

Alice's heart pounded.

Please don't look back at the car.

He didn't; but disappeared around the corner. She heard a car start but didn't dare move.

The car roared down the driveway but suddenly stopped and pulled into the circular driveway where the car Alice was driving was parked.

Her heart all but stopped.

Oliver left his car running but got out and walked up to the Mercedes SUV.

Alice peeked through the bush and watched as he took a picture of the license plate. He walked back to his car but stopped.

His car was gone!

Oliver froze for a minute, then turned around in circles several times. He spewed a string of profanity, looking like he had seen a ghost.

Alice suspected he had but didn't know it. She knew her family must be close by.

Oliver stood motionless, punching in numbers on his phone. He looked up when he heard a bike rolling toward him. The engine wasn't on, but it was rolling in his direction seemingly by itself.

The bike stopped next to him, and a set of keys fell at his feet.

The look on Oliver's face was pure fear, and at first, he did nothing.

He looked around, suddenly picked up the keys, and jumped on the bike. He sped out of the driveway, nearly dumping it when it hit the pavement. In seconds, he was out of sight.

Alice looked toward the door to make sure Joanne wasn't looking out. She ran to the driveway and got into her car.

"Hi, Mommy."

Alice screamed, "Audrey, you scared me to death!"

Alice was shaking so much she couldn't push the button to start the engine. Then she realized she didn't have her foot on the brake.

"Where are Daddy and Alex?"

Audrey sat up in the seat. She had been huddled under a blanket and now pointed out the window. "Right there."

James was just parking Oliver's car in the driveway, and he, Alex, and Tony got out and climbed in with Alice.

"Hurry, Alice. We need to get out of here," said Tony. He was punching numbers on his phone. Someone answered, and he said, "Yeah, he's on an all-black Harley; follow him, but don't intervene. Just find out where he's going."

Still shaking, Alice sped out of the driveway.

Suddenly she realized, "I forgot my purse! Oh no! He'll find it and know who I am!"

"Where is it, Mom?"

"On the porch on the side of the—wait, Alex, no!"

Before she even got the words out of her mouth, Alex leaped out of the car. In seconds, he was back, jumped in through the open-door Tony was holding for him, and said, "Here you go, Mom!"

"Go!" Tony yelled, scaring Alice, and she stomped on the gas. The car lurched forward, the tires screeching as she sped down the street.

"Wow! You do run fast!" Tony was visibly impressed as he gave Alex a high five.

"Oh my gosh!" Still shaking and talking too loudly, she looked at her husband, "How did you, why did you?"

James put his hand on her shoulder and pointed to her ear.

"You can slow down now." Tony was looking out the back window, "Don't go back to the hotel. We'll move you tonight."

"Did you forget about the earpiece? Tony could hear everything," said James.

Alice calmed down a little. She nodded, "I knew it was there, but I, yes, I guess I forgot." She shuddered, "Where are we going?"

"Let's get something to eat. Do you kids like fish?" asked Tony.

"We love fish." James smiled at Alice, "Good job."

She didn't look at him as tears welled up in her eyes.

"There's a great restaurant down by the water. My treat."

James laughed, "Your treat?"

"Well, I have to turn in the receipts," said Tony.

Alice parked the car and turned to look at James. "I did forget about the mic; I can't believe it."

"It's okay, you did fine."

Alex said, "What did you think, Mom, that we would hang you out to dry?"

Alice rolled her eyes, "Seriously? Where did you hear that?"

Alex shrugged, "I don't know."

They climbed out of the SUV, and Alice put her arm around Audrey. "You are getting so good at moving things with your mind! A car, a motorcycle? Wow!"

"But the most fun were the keys, huh Audrey?" said Alex.

Audrey laughed, "Yeah, you should have seen his face!"

The kids ran ahead, and Tony walked alongside Alice and James. She asked, "Could you hear the argument?"

"Not all of it," said Tony, "but we know where Oliver fits in now. You can fill us in tonight. Let's eat."

Linnea shook her shoulders when she and Thea morphed back into human form.

They had watched this exchange from a tree near the driveway where the Mercedes SUV was parked.

"Those are tough little kids," said Linnea.

"Agreed. Do the parents have any superpowers?" asked Thea.

"No, just the kids. The reason these parents must be here is the kids' ages. They're too young. That's what I was told."

They laughed, "I don't know; they seem to hold their own."

"Looks that way."

Linnea looked at the ground as the two walked to their waiting vehicle.

"What's on your mind?" asked Thea.

"I don't know if I like this assignment. They're kids."

"With superhuman powers, don't forget that. I'll bet they can give any of us a run for our money."

Linnea sighed, "You're right. What am I thinking?"

30

FANTASY ISLAND

GUNNER SAT IN SILENCE after listening to the report from Samual and Grant.

The two cousins looked at each other and then at Noelle and Haydee, sitting with them.

"I had a gut feeling about this, but I had no idea it would be so intense. They really are out to destroy all of you?"

Grant sighed. "It seems so. According to our contacts inside the military, the special forces mission is to destroy the Nessumsar family. It has to do with our great grandfather coming to America, never going back, and then decades later making it his mission to give all of us superhuman powers."

"We are endowed with them," said Haydee. "It's in our DNA; he couldn't give them to just anyone."

"The issue with the rivalry family, the Greblos family, is that our grandfather brought the superpowers to the United States, not so much that we have them," said Samual.

"So, if we moved to Norway, would we be, okay?" asked Noelle.

Samual shrugged, "I guess."

"Well, that isn't happening," said Haydee flatly.

"No kidding," Grant agreed.

"How many contacts did you say you have?" asked Gunner.

"They assigned us three. Two men and one woman. They don't know each other, nor do we know each other," said Grant. "One of us meets with one of them, individually."

Gunner looked surprised.

"It was your bosses who gave us the orders."

Gunner nodded, "I know."

"When we first brought Grandma to the Mayajaal all those years ago, she saw something. She told us about it just the other day," said Noelle.

"What was that?"

"Grandma said when Uncle Biorn took her up in the helicopter, she could see crows way off in the distance. But they didn't come close, and she said she felt safe here like they couldn't get to her."

"But the crows weren't trying to hurt her," said Samual.

"I get that; I was just wondering. We have never seen bats here, not ever. Maybe they can't get to Mayajaal. Maybe there is a protection—or something around the island."

"That's a possibility, right?" said Haydee.

Gunner scoffed, "With this group, anything is possible."

The four cousins laughed.

"That's the truth," said Samual.

"That's interesting, though, since these bats are apparently human," said Gunner.

Samual and Grant looked at each other, and then Grant said, "Not exactly."

"What? Are they not human? I just assumed they're like you and can change…"

"According to our sources, the special forces were all chosen because they are immortal. They can't be killed," said Samual.

"Well, that makes the playing field a little uneven," said Gunner.

"I was thinking *a lot* uneven," said Grant. "However, we were also told they were not trying to kill us. They are trying to deactivate our powers. That's it."

"But if they do kill you?"

Again, Grant and Samual exchanged a quick glance.

"That never came up," said Samual.

Dede opened the door and asked them, "Are you kids ever going to come in and eat? Your parents will be here soon."

"They'll be through in ten minutes." Gunner tapped the table with his knuckles and sighed heavily, "So much going on."

"Foods for you too, Gunner!" Dede closed the door.

Gunner took a deep breath, "I know you boys have been away from your families, but honestly, I can only give you tonight. I want to send the four of you to Belize tomorrow. I'm curious to see if the bats will find you there."

"So, we are like bait?" asked Noelle.

Gunner grinned, "Pretty much." He continued, "I may send you to the States; we'll see. I am not planning on it; a lot will depend on how things go in Belize."

"This mission we have everyone else assigned to is massive. Operation Purloin is our focus. It must be. Our government is depending on us. I just don't want any of your family getting destroyed by bats because we made you vulnerable." He pushed his fingers through his dark hair. "Bats, who would have guessed?"

"Oh," he added, "About the crows, bats, whatever, not getting to you here? I just wonder if there is any protection around the island. A barrier. What does Mayajaal mean?"

The four grinned.

"Magic, Illusion, Fantasy, to name a few," said Haydee.

Dede stepped up next to her grandkids, "It's priceless."

Gunner chuckled and looked around, "Your own Fantasy Island."

∽ 31 ∾

FINANCIAL EMPIRE?

ELEANOR ANDERSON started her pilfering computer scam in high school when she was fifteen. Later, when she played soccer in college, she continued to build her empire, mostly with college students. However, she found them unreliable, often going rogue, with a lack of discretion she couldn't tolerate. Due to some of their blunders, she had nearly been breached twice. She was not about to allow a third time.

It was then that she sought out the help of an old college professor, Jon Cutler, computer expert extraordinaire. He had left the college scene settling on a less stressful career teaching high school students how to use computers.

Four years into his career, Cutler met Steve Mercury, a fourteen-year-old freshman. Steve had one of the most brilliant computer minds Jon Cutler had ever encountered. It was Steve who came up with the concept of Praxis, the computer game that literally tricked players into stealing. Once the player was paid and hooked, that player was introduced to cyber theft; where the real money was, and where Geist stepped in with her expertise.

Eleanor had the funds to get the game underway, adding to Steve's remarkable understanding of the computer and gaming world, and Cutler's squeaky clean public persona, they rapidly put

133

their illegal business into seven-figure incomes. Under the code name Geist, Eleanor's had soared into the millions.

Cutler and Steve lived inconspicuous lives; no one would ever guess they had bankrolled so much cash. Eleanor, on the other hand, owned two mansions. One in San Jose, California, and the other in the Bahamas. With the amount of security around her, it was hard to get close. Up until six months ago, no one even tried. Geist, and her cohorts were running safely below the radar.

Then she made a fatal error.

Eleanor began recruiting school age children. She started with high school students, but then ventured into middle school and organized two highly successful middle school *clubs*. As far as the kids were concerned, they were simply playing a game and getting paid for it.

The genius behind the game they called Praxis, created by Steve, and expounded on by Eleanor were the subliminal messages being delivered to the participants whenever they played. Listening to the soundtrack while playing was a requirement. Each level had its own specifically coordinated soundtrack that included additional rules and instructions for that level. The subliminal messages were set to beats that coordinated with human brainwaves. Players were taught to keep secrets, to lie, to cheat, and a belligerent lack of respect for parents or teachers, all the while playing the *game*, and earning money.

Players would lose points or risk being demoted an entire level if they involved their parents even in conversation about the game. Tiny high-powered microphones embedded in the helmets monitored every sound the player made when wearing it. A later addition added a microphone on the outside of the helmet to eavesdrop on the players when they were in close proximity. This form of electronic brainwashing enabled the club leaders to easily control their constituents.

Each game was equipped with a unique password lock that made it impossible for anyone to penetrate the firewall without it. Praxis would lock itself after thirty minutes if the game was unattended.

Susan Cunningham, a thirteen-year-old middle school student fell asleep while playing Praxis. Her mother came in during the thirty-minute window. Out of curiosity, she put her daughter's headset on. She was shocked to hear some of the things Susan had been listening to, and even more appalled when she and Susan's father, learned how deep the subliminal messages penetrated their daughters' young brain.

Susan's parents called the police, which led to an FBI investigation. The depth of the organization and the sheer number of young people involved made it necessary to enlist the help of peers to crack the case—leading them directly to the seventeen cousins who lived and trained on Mayajaal.

The Nessumsar family agents were called in and assigned to schools in four states to work Operation Purloin.

❧ 32 ❦

GAMING HEAVEN

OLIVER WAS VISIBLY SHAKING when he walked into the vast living room. He had never been to the invisible Geist's home. He didn't know her real name and had never even seen a picture of her.

Oliver wasn't sure if the person he was following was a servant or butler; but he led him down a long winding staircase and through two separate sets of steel doors. Before entering the first one, he was searched and x-rayed.

Oliver stepped into a world beyond his wildest imagination through the second set of doors.

Thick plush wall-to-wall gray carpet and leather sofas strategically placed to enable a clear view of the dozens of gaming screens embedded in the walls. A raised, circular console in the middle of the floor had enough buttons and controls to run NASA, or so it seemed to Oliver.

Just under the screens and about two feet from the floor, a brilliant blue fish tank extended the entire length and width of the room on all four walls filled with many different varieties of Sealife. Oliver imagined the space to be about half the size of a basketball court, with much lower ceilings.

A bar in one corner offered an array of soft drinks, water, fruit juices, coffee, tea, and hot chocolate. Oliver felt like he had died and gone to gaming heaven.

They had been closed behind him but now opened again. Steve, Cutler, and Britt walked in.

"Oliver, good to see you." Cutler put an arm around his shoulder. He looked around, "What do you think of this little empire?"

"Starstruck, admit it," said Steve.

That was the most normal Oliver had ever seen Steve act.

"It is amazing, kind of hard to comprehend," said Oliver.

Britt hadn't even looked at him. "Hi Britt."

Britt nodded curtly but said nothing.

Cutler walked over to the bar, "Anyone want a soda?"

The door opened again, and a medium height, slender, woman entered the room.

"Are you entertaining in my gaming room, Jon?" she asked.

"Of course, isn't that my job?"

The woman rapidly covered the space between her and Jon and threw her arms around him.

"How are you, Ellie? I swear you haven't aged a day since college."

"Aww, thank you, Jon. I'm just great and excited for this day! I have been looking forward to it!"

Eleanor? Ellie? This was Geist?

Oliver was stunned.

The woman, although striking, was nothing he had expected. She had a softness about her the way her chin-length hair framed her face. She wore jeans, a long-sleeved t-shirt, and flip-flops. Her easy laugh was contagious.

She turned to face the group, "Steve, Britt, good to see you both again." She crossed the room again and gave each of them a hug.

Now, she turned to Oliver. She smiled, extended her arms, and took Oliver's hands. She smiled up at him; he was mesmerized by her clear green eyes.

"I am so happy to meet you, Oliver. You are an important person in this organization, our *clubs*," she smiled.

Steve coughed.

"Oh, not as important as you, Steve." She laughed and said to Oliver, "Steve always has to be reassured that he is most important to me!"

Steve chuckled, "I know I am."

Oliver was surprised to see Steve blush. That was a new one.

"Did they get you a nice hotel, Oliver?"

"Yes, the best. Thank you!"

"You're welcome," She turned to the other three, "You too, correct?"

They all nodded. "Of course, Ellie," said Cutler.

"Let's sit down for a minute. I'd like to go over our plans for tomorrow."

They all sat in a corner seating area on leather sofas. Oliver couldn't believe how soft they were.

"Thanks to all of you, of course, but for this past quarter, we have Oliver to thank for our overwhelming number and, might I add, quality recruits. I believe we have ten coming in tomorrow."

Oliver nodded, "Yep, ten."

"Each of these recruits has two or more under them and is growing as we speak," she smiled. "Now we know our elementary kids are not the actual recruits, but the game they play at their age is in preparation. Their mothers, however, benefit handsomely. I believe your own mother has had success."

"Stepmom. Stepmom," Oliver corrected her.

"Okay, I didn't realize."

"It's okay."

"Well, anyway, they are arriving in the morning. Our training is to teach them how to pay the players. Most of these kids do not have bank accounts, so we need them to learn the handoff method. This is crucial to the success of Praxis."

"Do I understand correctly that we will return to our own states for the handoff right?"

"Yes, but we don't have any training for the kids in the chain. They're paid to deliver; they do not play the game."

"Okay then, we'll see you here tomorrow."

Eleanor stood, and so did the other three. They followed her through the doors and up the stairs. She said goodnight and turned into another room.

Oliver arrived back at his hotel, still on cloud nine. He took a shower, ordered room service, and climbed into bed, dreaming of his own gaming heaven someday.

GAME OVER

ERIKKI AND NORA hung upside down from a Sycamore tree.

"I don't see how this is going to work."

"I know; look at this place swarming with the FBI." Nora nodded and sighed, "Well, let's see how it looks when they come out."

They glanced at each other, and Nora closed her eyes.

Erikki closed his eyes, too. *This is going to be impossible. I wonder what Sulo's message meant this morning. 'Be ready.'*

Be ready for what?

"We have to stay here till tomorrow—invisible?"

"Apparently," Spencer looked around. "It's not horrible; we only have to be invisible if someone is nearby."

"There are a million people here. How can one woman need so much help?" said Nate, then he added, "It was easier getting in here than I thought it would be."

"Yeah, I can't wait to see the gaming room."

"How lucky that the guy in Montana never met his recruiter face to face. Since the guy is in college, it will be easy for Harley to pass for him."

"You mean the one who's in jail?" asked Spencer.

"Yeah, that one."

Spencer yawned, "Let's get some sleep."

Morning came early. His recruits were exiting a stretch limo when Oliver got out of the car he was driven over in.

Cutler, Steve, and Britt arrived in a separate car.

When Harley filed past Nate and Spencer, though tempting, neither of them hit him like they had planned. They knew they needed to be discreet.

Harley was not carrying a weapon because he had to undergo screening, but Nate and Spencer brought theirs in through the open doors the day before when Oliver, Cutler, Steve, and Britt were leaving. Nate had Harley's gun and knew he needed to be near Harley to hand it off when taking them down.

He decided to move there now.

Eleanor Anderson entered, flanked by Oliver, Steve, and Cutler. Britt was already in the room.

Nate, Harley, and Spencer had been given strict orders: make no move until money is exchanged. Everything would be recorded through Nate and Spencer's ear mics and sunglass cameras.

Eleanor introduced herself. "I'm thrilled to have you all here today. I wanted you to see this room. I have a staff of twenty-five that monitor these computers twenty-four hours a day. Of course, except for the next half hour or so."

"You're here to be paid. After today, payment will be handled differently, but the first time, I would like to hand your cash to you myself. This is a celebration! You should be proud of yourselves!"

The recruits were mesmerized and obviously completely taken in by the overwhelming surroundings.

Eleanor continued, "Our largest payout today, covering the last four months, is one hundred and two thousand dollars. The smallest pay today is thirty-eight thousand. We hold this information in the strictest confidence and trust you will also."

Eleanor made her way around the room. She methodically handed each recruiter a gold envelope, shook their hand, and took a few minutes to talk with each one.

When finished, she walked to the front and asked, "Any questions?"

No one said anything.

Nate and Spencer both heard through their earpieces. "We're right outside the door. Go."

"I have a question," said Harley.

At that second, Spencer handed a nine-millimeter to Harley and pulled out his own. At the same time, he and Nate materialized, and the locks on the steel doors released.

FBI agents swarmed the room.

Harley dangled a pair of handcuffs in front of Eleanor, "I was wondering if these would fit."

Eleanor said nothing, her expression blank. She appeared speechless.

Major commotion ensued as the agents led Oliver's recruits up the stairs and out the mansion's front door, where police cars and vans awaited them.

Mack, Ava, and Micah joined Spencer on the front lawn.

Cutler glared at Mack when he passed them. Mack said nothing.

Oliver was crying, Steve was belligerent even in handcuffs, and Britt looked terrified.

Nate and Harley joined their cousins.

"One down," said Nate.

Now in handcuffs, Eleanor passed by them, escorted by two agents.

"The biggest one," said Spencer.

They all turned to see Char hurrying towards them.

She started to shake their hands, paused, and pulled the four into a group hug. "Well done, very well done. And without incident."

"Hey Nessumsars!"

They all turned in the direction of the voice; it was Eleanor. She pushed away from the agent who guided her into the backseat of the police car.

"It isn't over!" she yelled.

"Yes, it is!" Harley called back.

She laughed, "No, it isn't!"

The next thing that happened left the cousins and Char speechless.

Eleanor suddenly shrank, and the two startled agents next to her jumped back as she morphed into a starfish at their feet.

"What the…?" Mack started toward her.

"The tattoo! The starfish tattoo!" yelled Spencer, and he ran to catch up with Mack.

Harley, Micah, and Ava looked at one another in disbelief.

"I didn't see that coming!" Harley said what they were all thinking.

Suddenly, the starfish lifted off the ground, and Eleanor became a bat, stopping Mack and Spencer in their tracks.

The bat shot into the air but then streaked across the grass, swooping low enough to nearly hit Harley's head.

Deafening screeching filled the air and intensified when the bat flew toward the Sycamore tree.

Viewing the scene from their hidden location, Erikki and Nora were caught off guard when the unexpected bat flew directly at them and hovered. Her eyes locked first with Nora and then with Erikki.

Obediently, the two bats joined Eleanor, and the three darted away, leaving everyone on the ground in shock, including the Nessumsar cousins.

Still stunned, Erikki looked back at the baffled humans, and he and Nora stopped when Eleanor did.

She spun in the air and her steely black eyes locked with Harley's—then she abruptly shot straight into the air.

To be continued…

ABOUT THE AUTHOR

Author Debbie Ihler Rasmussen, author of *The Nessumsar Family— Legend of The Crow Series,* continues the adventure taking readers into a world of the paranormal, adventure, superhuman powers, and mystery.

Her greatest treasures are her six children and seventeen grandchildren, who now live in *four* states (That's new this year!)

This project is particularly close to Debbie's heart as it was for her grandchildren that these stories were originally written.

Raising six children who have families of their own, forty-four years of teaching dance, a lifetime of church service, random jobs, adventures, travel, and scores of treasured friends, add to her library of characters and ideas.

Imminence is the second book in the *Legend of The Crow Series,* where ancestors in Norway sought out and bestowed superhuman powers on their posterity in America, five generations later.

After thirteen years in Salt Lake City, Utah, Debbie made a quick decision in May of 2022 to move to Surprise, Arizona.

She loves the beautiful Arizona skies, monsoons, family, and her new *little* home in an awesome community. She loves all the seasons (but will probably not miss the snow—except on Christmas Eve); fall and spring are still her favorites.

Always giving thanks to God for the best family ever, amazing supportive friends, her health, and the blessing of writing. She loves (and misses) the beach, running (still walking), cycling, hiking, reading, and fun.

www.ingramcontent.com/pod-product-compliance
Lightning Source LLC
Chambersburg PA
CBHW060458300726
48975CB00008B/2555